THE COLONY OF SHADOWS

Bikram Sharma is from Bangalore. He completed an MA in Creative Writing from the University of East Anglia, and in 2016 he was awarded the Charles Wallace India Trust writing fellowship at the University of Kent. *The Colony of Shadows* is his debut novel.

THE COLONY OF SHADOWS

BIKRAM SHARMA

hachette
INDIA

First published in 2022 by Hachette India
(Registered name: Hachette Book Publishing India Pvt. Ltd)
An Hachette UK company
www.hachetteindia.com

1

Copyright © 2022 Bikram Sharma

Bikram Sharma asserts the moral right to be identified as the author of this work.

All rights reserved. No part of the publication may be reproduced, stored in a retrieval system (including but not limited to computers, disks, external drives, electronic or digital devices, e-readers, websites), or transmitted in any form or by any means (including but not limited to cyclostyling, photocopying, docutech or other reprographic reproductions, mechanical, recording, electronic, digital versions) without the prior written permission of the publisher, nor be otherwise circulated in any form of binding or cover other than that in which it is published and without a similar condition being imposed on the subsequent purchaser.

This is a work of fiction. Any resemblance to real persons, living or dead, or actual events or locales is purely coincidental.

Subsequent edition/reprint specifications may be subject to change, including but not limited to cover or inside finishes, paper, text colour and/or colour sections.

ISBN 978-93-93701-31-2

Hachette Book Publishing India Pvt. Ltd
4th & 5th Floors, Corporate Centre,
Plot No. 94, Sector 44, Gurugram 122003, India

Typeset in ITC Giovanni Std 10/14
by R. Ajith Kumar, New Delhi

Printed and bound in India
by Manipal Technologies Limited, Manipal

For my family

PROLOGUE

Ma and Pa's bedroom was empty. Their work clothes lay scattered across the floor, and perfume lingered in the hallway. It was eleven, the latest Varun had stayed up, and he knew Ma would give him a good shouting if she caught him prowling about at this hour, that too on a weekday. But it was quiet outside. He'd hear them the moment they returned.

He pocketed a coin Pa had left by the telephone and crept down the hallway into Ma's office. Her table was cluttered with blueprints, tubs of glue, and coils of glittery copper wire. On the floor was the cardboard gramophone they'd spent all evening making. Though the motor was disconnected from the battery, the air in the room still carried an electric charge. Ma had made him promise not to play with the gramophone because he could hurt himself, but he'd watched her closely and would be careful. He'd listen to only one song, maybe two. Plus, she'd broken her own promise of returning home early tonight.

He glanced at the window, half-expecting headlights to flash past as they pulled into the parking lot. But no, there was no sign of them. The darkness of the colony remained undisturbed. The clock in the hallway ticked on.

He connected the wires of the motor to the battery. The record wobbled, then revolved, its row upon row of concentric circles catching the light. He swivelled the arm across its spinning surface and eased the pin down. There was a scratch, a burst of static, and then there emerged from the depths of the horn the faintest stirrings of music. Sitting cross-legged on the cold floor, Varun waited for his parents to come home as he listened to the voices of ghosts plucked out of thin air.

1

Jyoti stood barefoot in the back garden and hung laundry on the clothesline. The grass was damp from the rain and the trees in the grove behind her rustled with every gust of wind. From the nearby construction site came the high-pitched whine of stonecutting, punctuated by drilling, hammering, blares of traffic, and the explosive hisses of pressure cookers from the adjacent apartment complex. She rubbed her forehead. There was no peace in this city. Development was relentless. Soon some enormous shopping centre would be leaning against their boundary walls and once again they'd be forced to debate whether or not they should just chuck everything and sell the place. It was a shame Varun couldn't experience the Bangalore of her youth. She carried the laundry basket back inside the house.

In the kitchen, Seema was stirring masala, which sizzled. Jyoti brushed past her and slid the laundry basket under the counter. 'Is my mother awake?'

'No.'

'Very nice. She's going to end up sleeping through the entire day.'

'I'll clean her room? It hasn't been done for so long.'

Jyoti pressed a button on her phone and listened to the automated voice state the time. 'No, it's too late. Leave it.'

Sliding her hand along the walls, she headed for the guest bedroom but stumbled into a stool. She winced at the flare of pain in her shin. She needed to remind Varun that in this house he couldn't leave stuff all over the place. Poor thing. All these new rules.

'Varun?' She knocked on his open door. 'Varun?'

There was a flurry of movement, the scrape of a chair. 'Hi, Jyoti Aunty.'

'What are you doing?'

'Homework.'

'Are you sure?'

'Yeah.'

'Promise?'

'I... yes.'

She sat on his bed, patted the bedcover, and found Lego pieces and something larger that he'd been building. Balancing it on her palm, she traced its shape with her fingertips.

'An aeroplane?'

'It's not yet finished.'

She twirled the propellers attached to its wings and felt a painful catch in her chest. Anu would've been so proud.

'And your homework?'

'It's also not yet finished.'

'Okay, well, maybe you could do that first, and then we could unpack your boxes? There are still three left, no?'

The boxes were stacked on top of each other by his wardrobe and she was keen to strike them off the to-do list. It would help, she imagined, to have his clothes fill the wardrobe, his drawings hang from the walls, and his toys litter the floor. Maybe then he would feel more comfortable here.

'Can I go outside?' he asked.

'Weren't you just now saying your homework isn't finished?'

'I don't even have school.'

'I've told you, you have to keep practising. Otherwise, things will be extra difficult when you rejoin classes. This is important.'

'Just for a short while. Please?'

There was such eagerness in his voice. She remembered playing a game with him when he was a baby, small for his age yet heavy in her arms. She would place him inside his crib and hide her face behind her hands. His agitation would grow, and just when it seemed like he was on the verge of crying, she would re-emerge with a whoop. How he spluttered with delight. *Where's your Jyoti Aunty? Here she is! Yes, here she is!* Disappear, reappear, disappear, reappear. What limitless joy he took from the game, from the moment of her return.

'Okay. You can go play. But,' the chair scraped back, 'make sure you come back for lunch and don't get caught in the rain and please be careful okay?'

He was already thudding his way out.

How had Anu managed? In their conversations, her sister always mentioned classes and after-school activities like swimming, trips to heritage sites, and fun little experiments in engineering. And yet, here she was, struggling to make him follow a bare-bones timetable. A month had passed and she still didn't know what to do with him. What would happen when she went back to work?

She set the aeroplane down. It was a feat of imagination like the origami she and Anu used to make when they were children, or the paper boats they launched across puddles. Back then they loved embarking on adventures in the grove. They pretended to be fearless discoverers, though their bravery deserted them every time they returned home late to find Mama frothing at the mouth with worry.

She reached for her cane by the front door. Perhaps it would be best to bring him back and have him focus on homework for now. Keep him safe. But she hesitated. After she lost her vision, there were no more games or adventures in the grove. She was forbidden from entering it. *How will you go?* Mama asked. *All those thorns and roots. Who will help you walk between trees, huh? One trip, one fall, then I'll be the one rushing you to the hospital to take care of your broken bones.*

She tapped the floor with her cane. Maybe being in a constant state of worry was what it meant to be a parent, and maybe climbing trees or playing hide-and-seek with the shadows was what Varun needed right now. Some time and space. Let him be, she convinced herself. It would be good for him to explore. And where was the harm? It wasn't like he was going to vanish without a trace.

2

Varun walked through the grove behind the bungalow. He'd spent the past week counting the trees on the property and only recognized three. At the end of the driveway was the massive banyan, hundreds of roots dangling from its branches and weaving into one another to form delicate curtains he could brush aside. By the side of the house was the guava tree. Even though Jyoti Aunty had warned him to be careful, he'd still scraped his elbows climbing its trunk. And the guava he plucked was so hard he couldn't even bite into it. Poppy had sniffed the guava without interest, then chased after a squirrel and barked as it scurried across branches. The third and final tree was the most special. A bougainvillea in bloom by the boundary wall. Ma's favourite. Sometimes they would go for a walk in the colony's park and she would point at trees and ask him to guess their names. Bougainvillea had been the easiest to learn because of how difficult it was to spell. Who knew a word could hide so many letters? Ma had laughed the first time he guessed at its spelling.

The smell of wet earth was rich this deep inside the grove, with its muddy puddles and leaves turning to mulch. It reminded him of rain on stone, of Ma's hands after gardening.

It was winter in Delhi. His school sometimes closed for days because of the pollution, and he and Komal liked to sit in front of the television and watch cartoons all day long, warming their feet against the portable heater. Outside, a dense fog would hang low among the tree branches, coating the roofs of parked cars with moisture.

In Bangalore, there was no fog. The air was light, bright, and not even that cold. Peering through the gaps in the canopy, he could see kites flying in graceful circles, their wings spread wide and their bodies dipping with the wind. How did they do that? He would have to look this up when he got home. Then he remembered home was packed into suitcases and cardboard boxes. He didn't even know if they'd brought Ma's nature books or Pa's gigantic leather-back volumes of Indian history. What about the gramophone?

The back of his throat prickled. He kicked at a tree trunk. The sight of its scraped bark immediately made him whisper an apology.

No, the boxes in his room only contained his old belongings, not theirs. Maybe there were other boxes hidden away, but Jyoti Aunty was so keen to unpack and shelve and tidy up that he would've noticed. There was always something she wanted him to do.

He pinched himself. It wasn't fair to think cruel thoughts about her. Ma had told him that Jyoti Aunty faced difficulties he could never understand. He picked up a stick and, keeping his eyes shut, tapped the ground and moved forward with an arm outstretched. He tripped over a root. He splashed into a puddle and soaked one of his shoes. His sock squelched with every step. He tripped over another root and stumbled headfirst into a wall.

Here he was, struggling to walk a few feet. Meanwhile, Jyoti Aunty could cross roads without hesitation.

He removed his shoe and squeezed the water from his sock. The wall he'd walked into was the boundary wall, and from the other side came the incredibly loud sounds of construction. There were great booms and hoarse calls. He wasn't sure what was happening out there, but clouds of dust drifted over the wall and settled on the leaves and branches of the grove. Following the boundary wall, he caught sight of the bougainvillea and tried to recall what Ma had told him. *The vines have long, spiky thorns, so be careful! The flowers are actually white but they're surrounded by a cluster of pink leaves called bracts.*

What else?

Above him, shards of glass from broken bottles had been wedged into the cement at the top of the boundary wall.

What else had Ma told him? How could he have forgotten so much? The last time they went for a walk in the park, he'd ditched her for a game of seven stones without even saying goodbye.

He remembered Pa plucking bougainvillea near Feroz Shah's tomb and threading it through her hair. And the jar in the living room, which she liked to fill with small pebbles and delicate pink bracts. And the time when she bandaged his fingers after he pricked himself on their thorns and was surprised into tears.

But he couldn't remember anything else Ma had told him about bougainvillea.

He rested his forehead against the wall. Its surface was grainy, browned over the years with plenty of cracks and chips. It looked like it could collapse from the slightest of touches. He half-wished it would.

Voice tight in his throat, he whispered, 'I want to go home.'

The wall gently shook with the pounding of construction. The movement disturbed a lizard from its hiding place. Varun watched it skitter across the wall. It was pale green and so translucent that he could see veins branching beneath its skin. Pa was terrified of lizards. *The way they move! Yikes! Why are they so unpredictable, man?* He would flee from the room while Ma, laughing, would nudge the lizard into a cup to set it free in the colony's park.

'Hello, little ghost,' Varun said, just as Ma used to say. He offered his open palm to the lizard, but it disappeared down a hole in the wall. Kneeling to get a better look, he was surprised to find the hole was large enough that he could squeeze through. On the other side were a filthy courtyard and an empty swimming pool.

Varun frowned. He'd expected to see blue tarpaulin sheets and bamboo scaffolding, piles of sand and cement mixers. Not an empty swimming pool. Where were the construction workers? Everything was carpeted in a thick layer of dust. Filthy and drained of water, the swimming pool looked strange. Like it didn't belong there. And yet there was something familiar about it.

He thumbed the edges of the hole, the wall's insides with its mossy bricks that were powdery yet rough to the touch. If he wanted to, he could cross over. He could have a quick look around and be back on this side without anyone knowing. He could. There was no one to stop him. Grandma hardly left her bed and Jyoti Aunty never stepped inside the grove. Even if Jyoti Aunty did wander past this spot, it wouldn't matter because she couldn't see.

His neck burnt with shame. No, that was not nice. He shouldn't have thought that. Picking at a scab on his elbow, he considered going back to the house to finish his homework, maybe help Jyoti Aunty unpack the remaining boxes. But then he spotted something inside the pool. It was small, circular, casting a shiny speck of a reflection. A coin. Waiting to be found.

Varun glanced over his shoulder, then squeezed through to the other side. Seconds later, the hole in the wall sealed itself up.

3

Poppy twitched her nose. The hairs on her back stood on end, bristly as thorns. She could smell it in the wind, sense it in the air. Something was very wrong. There had come a swift predatory sound from the grove, like a cat leaping to snatch a pigeon, crushing a windpipe between its teeth and muffling panicked wingbeats by clawing flesh.

She pawed the front door.

'You want to go out?' her sister asked.

She barked.

'Okay, okay, no need to be so noisy.' Her sister slid her hand along the wall and guided herself to the front door, which she opened.

Poppy padded out and listened. The insects in her territory had gone deathly quiet. She sniffed the grounds around the house, seeking the source of this disturbance, and soon picked up the scent of the boy.

Sweat.

Stone.

Blood.

She sneezed.

Grief.

The last one was potent, like orange rinds turning rancid in the summer. She'd grown accustomed to it hanging thick and oppressive inside the house, especially over her poor ma, but here it was, spilt outside.

She lowered her nose to the ground and followed the boy's scent. Along the way he'd stumbled. Had he used a stick? Here was a scuffed trunk, here a shallow puddle, and his tracks. Her apprehension mounted as she moved away from the outer rings of her territory into hostile underbrush. Several times she heeded the warning calls of birds and took off, only resuming her search when she was sure she wasn't being watched. She kept expecting a scene of violence, feathers and blood. Just as she was beginning to tire, her joints stiff and aching, she arrived at the boundary wall where the boy's scent winked out.

Gone.

Vanished.

And in its place stood a vertical line of darkness, hissing and crackling at the edges.

Poppy yelped and scurried away. She hid behind a tree and sniffed the earth, the roots. A tunnel! How was this possible? She'd always believed they were stories told to pups to warn them of the pipes under the city. What was this, then? How was she supposed to defend her territory against something that was like waves of heat trembling on the horizon? This was no prey that could be savaged by her teeth.

Where was the boy? The boy, the boy! This was his doing, climbing over boundaries without sensing the danger lying in wait.

She thought about leaving. She could go back to the house, eat her rice and mince and laze in the garden, or maybe walk her sister up and down the driveway and then lie under the blanket beside her ma. It would be so easy to go back.

Safety, comfort, family.

And what if something happened to the boy? He was still only a pup. He was not like that man who'd treated her so roughly. The family had suffered enough. With the boy lost, their grief would turn solid, climb upon their shoulders, and wrap its hands around their throats.

Her sister whistled from home. 'Poppy! Where are you? Food's ready.'

The timing was cruel, like a vet's injection sliding under pinched fur. But wasn't that life? It was capable of breathtaking cruelty, striking from out of nowhere, random, unrepentant, leaving devastation in its wake or little children at the mercy of grief. Poppy was no fool. She knew the truth. To go would be to abandon the boy, and the boy was under her protection.

What was she to do, then?

The answer came from instinct. Poppy began to dig.

4

Varun walked across the courtyard, leaving behind him a trail of shoeprints. He tried to make as little noise as possible. The last thing he wanted was some watchman grabbing his wrist and dragging him back to the bungalow. It would be awful explaining himself to Jyoti Aunty. He'd never seen her angry, though he'd heard her arguing with Grandma. Unlike Ma and Pa, who maintained silence and distance during fights, Jyoti Aunty and Grandma would lock themselves in a room and shout at each other, their voices turning loud and unfamiliar.

He stood by the shallow end of the swimming pool. There were faded numbers on both sides indicating the depths. The metal stairs that normally dipped inside water now hung in mid-air, rusted orange. The bottom of the pool was filthy, and its tiles were either broken or missing. Pa would've loved this place. *In many ways, beta, there's a charm to erosion. To see what's destroyed, and what's left behind.*

The coin was in the deep end.

He climbed down and couldn't help but smile. It was strange to move so freely in a pool, without any resistance, and he pretended to freestyle down the middle, his arms cutting through invisible water. He bent to pick up the coin. It was a 50 paisa, the same kind that Pa would toss into the pool before they held their breath and dived underwater, sliding their palms along the floor in a race to find it first.

What was it doing here?

The pool was in the centre of the courtyard. The boundary wall ran along one side, and on the other side lay the ruins of a small pavilion. Its roof had collapsed, bringing down the walls. A broken pillar stood among the rubble like a headstone. Towering above him was a concrete diving board. Varun remembered the rush of falling from a great height, Pa's arms wrapped around him as their bodies plunged into the water. Ma would sit in the shade of the pavilion, drinking coffee and reading while he and Pa played in the pool. Sometimes they splashed water on her to hear her shriek. Varun was still learning to swim. He liked holding his breath for as long as possible, watching others glide by or Pa's hairy belly jiggle towards him. Even underwater he could hear himself laugh. The rubber floats Pa insisted he wear gave him rashes, and any opportunity he got he would slip them off and swim without worry, knowing that within seconds Pa's palms would steady him.

He put his hand on his chest.

It was as if this pool was the same one in which he'd learnt to swim. Except it was in Bangalore now instead of Delhi. And in ruins.

'How?' he asked the tiles.

How? How? How?

He gasped at the echo. It was so quiet here. He hadn't noticed it before, but now the silence seemed to take on a physical presence.

'Hello?'

Hello? Hello? Hello?

'HELL-O!'

HELL-O? HEll-o? Hell-o?

The silence rearranged itself around him. He couldn't even hear the sounds of construction. What was going on?

Wishing Pa was here to lift him on to his shoulders, he ignored the patter of his footsteps as he walked back to the shallow end and climbed out of the pool. He pocketed the coin. If he was smart and careful, he could continue to explore this place for another ten minutes, maybe fifteen, and then hurry back to the bungalow. Jyoti Aunty and Grandma would never know he'd been here. No one would. Although, he realized, his footprints were proof that he'd trespassed. Still, there was no need to worry. This place was empty.

Or was it?

He twisted. There was no movement in the courtyard. He turned. There was no movement in the pavilion. Maybe his imagination was playing tricks, but he felt certain that someone was watching him.

'Hello?'

The only place where someone could be hiding was within the ruins of the pavilion. He stared into its shadows, waiting for the face of an old watchman to emerge and croak threats. But nothing happened. Then he heard a scuffling. Wide-eyed, he turned towards the wall and saw that the hole he'd crawled through was gone. Gone! But how? Where was it? The scuffling sounds were getting closer and closer. Before he could do anything, a small patch of earth crumbled at the base of the wall to reveal the white snout of a dog.

'Poppy?'

She pulled herself out of the ground. Her ears were flat, her eyes bright. She was panting and threads of saliva fell from her jaws.

'Poppy!'

His mouth stung like he'd pressed his tongue against a battery. There was movement behind him. A shadow glided across the courtyard floor. Poppy snarled. And a voice whispered in his ear, Look.

Varun yelped and scrambled towards the wall, searching desperately for the hole. How could it have vanished? It had to be here. It had to!

With a swoop of horror, he felt a tug at his shirt. He yanked himself free.

Poppy's barks were deafening.

Blood thundered in his ears and all he wanted was to get out of there, to get back to the bungalow, and then he saw the hole! It was behind Poppy, who was baring her teeth. Scooping her into his arms, he dived through the hole, scraping his shoulders against the edges but not caring about the pain. His skin burst into goose pimples as something grabbed at his legs, clutched at his shoes, but then he was through, on the other side, back in the grove with construction roaring behind him, stumbling over tree roots as he raced to put as much distance between himself and the wall.

5

Poppy didn't stop running till she reached the back garden and the scents of her territory. The boy collapsed, out of breath. She tried to calm down. There were no signs of danger and they were safe now, but her body remained unconvinced. She snapped at the air. There was no explaining the revulsion. She rolled across the ground, coating herself with mud, leaves, fleas, and the things of this earth.

Wretched boy! Never trust a male and their mischief.

But she spared him her anger. He was sitting with his head between his knees, breathing in shallow gasps. His body reeked of rancid oranges and something else, sharp yet sickly sweet. Confusion? She shook herself upright. The boy was to blame, no doubt, but he was also just a pup. She sniffed his ankles, his shins, then licked his ear.

'Hi, Poppy.'

She allowed him to stroke her head. She could sense him returning to the present, though he peered through the grove towards the tunnel. She did the same, afraid she might hear the hiss and crackle. But there were only the sounds of construction.

A tunnel. An actual tunnel. And she'd dug her way through to the other side. How many dogs could make the same claim? Certainly not that useless retriever down the road, which was all bark and no brains. Nor that yapping Pomeranian with its stupid false bravado. She'd arrived just in time. The boy had been so clueless. So reckless! But it didn't matter anymore. They were safe. She wanted to hurry back inside and tell her sister and her ma.

The boy stood up. His legs trembled. She watched him in case he toppled over, but no, he was okay, tottering a bit and then heading away from home and back towards the boundary wall.

Oaf!

Fool!

Idiot!

Mischief maker!

'Shh, Poppy, give me a second,' he said, asking for time when he didn't even understand the laws of that place, how it existed outside of time, where mere seconds could still into an eternity. No! Enough was enough! Why were males always so self-destructive? She nipped at his socks, ripping stitches and stretching elastic. When that didn't work, she barked as loudly as she could.

'Shh, Poppy. Good dog.'

No!

No!

No!

No!

At last, he held his hands up. 'Okay, okay, Poppy. Sorry.'

She stiffened her tail and kept it upright, only wagging it when he reached out to brush the dirt off her back and remove a twig caught in her ear.

'I'll stop. See?' he said. 'And thank you for helping me.'

She twitched her nose. The boy was a dangerous brew of

grief spiked with fear, but his apology had the sincerity of a butter biscuit. She relaxed. For now. She led him towards the front door, and as she did, a lightness zipped through her body, her muscles, and she darted between bushes, sleek and agile like a pup claiming her first territory.

A tunnel. She couldn't wait to tell her ma.

6

Jyoti tried to focus on preparing for next week's classes, but she was too distracted by Poppy barking her head off in the garden. She rubbed her forehead. It was impossible to concentrate on work with her mind pulled in so many different directions. Varun, Mama, returning to the AFB, her grant application, the bills, the stupid checklist, Praveen's messages, and wanting to go to Tara's art studio to finally learn how to use a kiln. Where was the time?

She set aside her laptop just as the front door opened. Poppy scrabbled inside, panting away, and was followed by Varun, who scraped grit with his every step as he tried to shush her.

'Wait!' she called out, heading for the hallway. 'Are your shoes dirty or clean?'

'... Dirty, Jyoti Aunty.'

'So, Seema just swabbed the floors. Why don't you take off your shoes and leave them by the doorway?'

There was a pause as he struggled out of them, and then he hurried past her.

'Remember to wash your hands, please. Then you can have your snack. And maybe then we can tackle some of those boxes!'

Thinking it best to clean his shoes now before the mud

hardened, she stooped to pick them up. They were so small. Tracing the soles, she imagined Varun's footprints on the floor, evaporating, vanishing, and she thought about how her sister would never again measure his height.

He's growing up so fast, Anu had said over the phone.

These gentle moments crept up on her with such astonishing force. A spindle rotated within her ribcage, twisting sinew and muscle into something too unwieldy for her to carry. She staggered to the back of the house and rinsed his shoes with the garden hose. Her pulse refused to settle. Dizzy, she braced herself against the side of the house and whispered, 'Come on.'

Seema was cooking chicken stew and the air was laced with star anise and cinnamon. She needed to pull herself together. She went in. The kitchen was warm from the stove and Seema was bustling about. She peeled a papaya, sliced it in half, spooned out its slippery seeds, and cut the fruit into cubes. She took the bowl to the dining table and called Varun.

He scraped back a chair beside her. As he ate, clinking his fork against the bowl, she said, 'Next time, make sure you clean your shoes. I'll leave a bucket and sponge for you outside. All you have to do is just wipe the sides and soles.'

'Sorry.'

'No need to say sorry. Seema is busy with housework and it's not fair if you get mud all over the place. You keep your bedroom tidy, so this shouldn't be too difficult, right?'

He didn't say anything.

She fidgeted with the table mat. Maybe she was being too strict. Forcing him to follow too many rules. He was just a boy.

'Did you have a fun time playing outside?'

'You know how Poppy is called Poppy?' he asked.

'Yes.'

'And you know how Poppy sounds like Papaya?'

'Um, yes?'

'Do you think her dog name is Papaya?'

'Her dog name?'

'Like her dog age. Grandma said Poppy's at least nine, which means she's… sixty-five in dog years. I think? The first year is twenty-five, and each year after that is five. I read that in one of Ma's books.'

'So, if Poppy has a dog age, she has a dog name and a dog life?'

'Yes. Right?'

Jyoti tried not to laugh at how serious he sounded. 'That's probably the best way to think about it, yes. But if you're asking me how Poppy got her name, well, the story behind that is very boring. Your grandmother read it in one of your grandfather's old books. Poppy is probably named after some dusty old Victorian heiress.'

'Oh,' he said, sounding unimpressed.

He finished eating his papaya and took the bowl and fork to the kitchen. Seema told him to leave them in the sink, but he said it was okay, it would take him only a second to wash them. Water gushed from the tap. Seema thanked him with a chuckle. Soon he was back, sitting next to her but not saying a word.

'Why so quiet? What're you thinking about?'

'Do your hands hurt?' he asked.

'My hands? No. Why?'

He took her right hand, laid it on the table, palm upwards, and traced the cuts on her fingertips and the welt on her wrist.

'Oh. They're from cooking. Don't worry, it happens all the time. Even Seema has a few of these battle scars.'

'Is it… don't you find it difficult to cook?'

'No. I learnt how to do it a long time ago. At the AFB.'

'So, someone showed you how to use a knife and rolling pin and all that other stuff?'

'Yes.'

'But what about the stove?'

'I learnt how to use pretty much everything in the kitchen. It's easy. I can teach you if you want. My teacher back then was this lady called Hema. She's the principal now. Very strict! Very prim and proper. She made sure we knew how to take care of ourselves and she wouldn't allow anyone to mope. There were other classes I had to take as well.'

'Like maths?'

'Sort of. I mean, of course, there were classes on maths and science and geography, but there were also a lot of practical workshops. Things like carpentry, electronics, learning to read braille. You know my friend, Aunty Zarina? She taught me how to use a computer.'

'I never had any of those classes.'

'Right, but why would you?'

'Will I be going to the AFB?'

'Oh… no, Varun. It's an all-girls school. And it's the Association for the Blind. You'll be going to a school nearby.'

He was silent.

'Are you worried about going to a new school?'

'No.'

'I know how difficult it can be. I experienced the same thing when-'

He scraped back his chair. She lost him for a few seconds, then heard the door to his room creak shut.

So, yes, a little bit worried about joining a new school.

But that was no surprise. Change was scary. When she lost her sight, she too took to locking herself up in her room. Blindness made her speak loudly. After Mama shushed her in front of guests for apparently shouting the house down, she decided never to speak again. Best to keep her mouth shut till she died. How horrible those nights were, crying into her pillows and asking herself the same questions again and again. Why me? What's wrong with me? What's wrong with Mama and Papa and their genes? What did I do to deserve this? Why not Anu instead?

She went to the bathroom to splash cold water on her face.

At the AFB, she and the other teachers were responsible for helping students manage their fear. But what of grief? Varun was quiet and polite in front of her, doing as asked, but he was no longer the boy from before the accident, the boy who climbed people's shoulders or burst into rooms shouting for attention.

She wiped her face dry.

Hopefully, in time that boy of old would return.

1

Sitting at his study table, Varun peeled back his sleeve to inspect his shoulder for bruises. Nothing yet, though when he pressed his thumb against the skin it felt tender. Maybe the skin would purple. He wouldn't mind. His old school nurse pretended to chide him and call him 'wounded warrior' whenever she dabbed iodine over his scrapes.

He was confused. What was that place? And who had spoken? Why had they tried to grab him? He'd only just managed to escape.

Even with the windows closed, he could hear the sounds of construction. But the place beyond the wall had been so silent. He and Pa had been enveloped by a similar hush when they'd entered Feroz Shah's tomb. Through the holes of an arch, he'd glimpsed snatches of the world outside. Pigeons wheeling through the bright blue sky, the glimmering leaves of a neem tree. Pa had cupped his chin and raised his face to the domed ceiling, pointing out geometric lines rising from the arches to intertwine and loop around a red circle bordered with white calligraphy.

Beautiful, no?

It was.

Such harmony. The inscriptions are verses from the Quran. They're hundreds of years old. Can you imagine? But see what happens.

Some visitors had signed their names or left messages on the white marble cenotaphs in the centre of the chamber. One message scrawled in capital letters and red ink was full of bad words.

I don't understand, beta. Where does it come from, this hate?
Not knowing what to say, he'd held Pa's hand.

'Pa,' Varun whispered to his sheet of homework. He closed the door to his bedroom, lay on his bed, and pushed his face into his pillow.

8

Late in the evening, Jyoti smelled the rain before it fell and hurried to close all the windows. By the time she reached the living room, it was coming down and gusts of wind sprayed mist through the house. The floors were already slippery. Thankfully she wasn't stuck outside in this weather. She gasped. The clothes!

Grabbing her cane, she called out, 'Varun! Varun? Help me, please.'

His door opened. 'Jyoti Aunty?'

'We need to get the clothes.' She opened the front door and within seconds was drenched. How stupid! This was exactly the type of nonsense Mama used to make her and Anu do when they were children. Anu would complain that the clothes were already wet, what was the big deal in just leaving them, and Mama would threaten to beat them black and blue if they didn't hurry. Jyoti had sided with her sister back then. Yet here she was, unclipping heavy towels and draping them over her shoulder like a lunatic.

'The thing has fallen over,' Varun said.

'What thing? The clothes rack?'

'Yeah.'

'The clothes rack fell over?'

'Yeah.'

'Perfect. And what about the clothes?'

'They're in the mud.'

'Pick them up, quickly!'

'I've got them.'

'Okay, let's go back. It's really coming down.'

Inside the house, they both squelched about ruining the floors. So much for her lecture on being tidy and responsible. Seema was gone for the day, which was probably for the best because otherwise she would've been miffed.

'Thanks,' she said, taking the clothes from him. 'Switch on the geyser. Give it ten minutes and then you can take a nice hot shower.'

'Do we need to get anything else from outside, Jyoti Aunty?'

'Don't be silly.'

He chuckled. She listened to him walk down the hallway till the rain swallowed his footsteps. He'd sounded self-important, happy. She supposed dashing through the rain was a form of physical release. Maybe she should once again introduce him to some of the boys in the neighbourhood and see if they all wanted to play cricket. Would he want that though? Her past few attempts had ended in awkward silences and him staying close to her. It was difficult to make friends in a new city. So many connections had been severed. Sometimes the landline would ring and it would be Komal, the little girl who was his neighbour in Munirka. So sweetly she spoke. Yet Varun wouldn't answer Komal's calls, pretending to be busy or running out and leaving her to apologize to the poor girl. What she needed, she thought, dumping the soaked laundry on the kitchen counter, was for Mama to get up and help. At least between the two of them, they could find time to help Varun adjust. She wrung out the towels. Water dribbled into the sink.

'Hopeless.'

There was a boom, followed by a crackle of thunder. The hum of electricity died in the kitchen. The fridge switched off. Seconds later, the generator turned on, then sputtered out. It whirred, clicked, and gave up.

'Hopeless,' she said again. Maybe the geyser had tripped it. Or maybe it was useless like all the other ancient devices in the house which needed replacing. She took out her phone and added 'call electrician' to her checklist.

'Varun! I'll boil some water for you, okay? You can take a bucket bath instead.'

'Jyoti?' Mama called out from her room.

'Oh! You're finally awake?'

'Obviously, no? It's raining. Did you bring the clothes in?'

Jyoti ignited the stove. Cursing power cuts and sleeping mothers, she went to change into some dry clothes. It felt good to wear something that didn't cling to her body. When she returned to the kitchen, the water was boiling, bubbling, overflowing, and hissing as it spilt into the flame. She turned off the gas, wrapped one of the soaked towels around the steel vessel, and carried it to the guest bedroom.

No. That wasn't right, she reminded herself. Not the guest bedroom but Varun's bedroom.

'Varun?'

Curtains of steam enveloped her face as she poured the hot water into a bucket and scalded the tip of her thumb. Wincing, she shouted his name. Where was he? She couldn't hear him. The bedroom was filled with the sound of rain.

'Varun? Are you here?'

'Hi, Jyoti Aunty.' He was standing by the windows.

'What're you doing?'

'Nothing.'

'There's hot water in the bucket.'

He didn't say anything.

'You... do you want me to show you how to mix the water to the right temperature?'

'I know how to do that.'

'Okay. Then what's the problem?'

Again, he didn't say anything.

Uncertain what to say or do, she kept quiet and waited by the doorway for what felt like an eternity before he at last spoke again, this time in a whisper that barely carried.

'Sorry, what did you say?'

'It's dark in the bathroom.'

It was strange to consider the darkness as frightening, as she'd been living in shades of it for so many years. But he was just a child. And he'd spent an entire night in Munirka alone, waiting for Anu and Alok to come back.

'Come with me,' she said, offering her hand. He took it, his hand so small in her own, and she led him to the kitchen. 'Next time there's a power cut, you go to the kitchen and open the topmost drawer closest to the door. Go on, open it. What do you see?'

The wooden drawer rasped open. 'Coasters?'

'What else?'

'Nothing else.'

'Look carefully.'

He rummaged about. 'Oh. Candles?'

'And there should be a matchbox.'

'Found it.'

'Good. Bring the matchbox and a candle, but don't light anything. They're not for playing, you understand?'

He squeezed her hand.

'Good.'

They returned to the bedroom. With a firm strike of a match, she lit a candle.

'You hold the match like this and angle it away from you. Don't play with the fire and don't let it get too close to your fingertips. Once you've lit the candle, blow out the match,' she said, demonstrating as she spoke. She carried the candle into the bathroom, poured a blob of wax on to the rim of the sink, and then balanced the flame on the porcelain. 'Better?'

'Yeah.'

'If you want, you can keep the bathroom door open. That way there's light coming in through the windows as well. What do you think?'

'Okay.'

She left the bathroom door wide open and the bedroom door ajar. Soon the hallway filled with the sound of water gushing from the tap. She waited there the whole time he bathed, folding and refolding his damp clothes, listening in case he called for her. But she doubted he would. He'd acted self-consciously, standing by the windows, shying away from the darkness but not telling her why. Did he feel like a stranger around her?

When he finished bathing, she retreated to the kitchen to give him some privacy. She heated up the chicken stew Seema had cooked, garnished it with diced coriander, and rolled dough into rotis and fluffed them up over the tawa. For Mama, she prepared a plate of cold curd rice.

Inside Mama's room was a strong smell of powdery medicine tablets, dog fur, and oniony body odour. 'Here, Mama.' She sat down on the bed and handed her the plate.

'What's this? Oh...'

She could hear the disappointment in Mama's voice and was content. 'Curd rice. You were complaining about how your stomach has been so sensitive these past few days and preventing you from getting out of bed.'

'I thought I smelled something else.'

'Seema made chicken stew. Varun and I are eating that.'

Mama hummed. She always did when dissatisfied. 'I can't have any pickle? What is this, Jyoti? There aren't even any curry leaves or mustard seeds.'

'Sorry, Mama. I thought it best to play it safe.'

She listened to Mama scrape the plate with her spoon. Poppy lay next to her, burying her snout under her thigh. She patted the dog's back. Outside, it continued to pour.

'These power cuts,' Mama said, 'they remind me of Anu.'

Jyoti sighed.

'I went with her to Delhi when she first moved, do you remember? It was June. The weather was insufferable. Such heat! We kept the AC running full blast the entire time I was there. One day the air became so stuffy it was like inhaling cotton. It rained that evening. You know what the weatherman said? It was the-'

Heaviest rainfall in thirteen years.

'-heaviest rainfall in thirteen years. The city came to a standstill. There were power cuts, just like this one. We were sweating buckets. And then, can you believe it, Anu went and built an inverter. Out of nothing! Some wires and some plastic boxes. It didn't carry a huge charge, but we could at least run the portable fan. She did it all by herself. It was no big deal for her, but that day I told myself, yes, she will be okay.'

How many times had Jyoti heard this story? It never failed

to set her teeth on edge. That first year, Mama had publicly celebrated Anu's employment at a renowned engineering firm. She also seized any opportunity she got to pour disdain over Jyoti's Sociology degree. But what she didn't know was that Anu called Jyoti late every night to vent about how much she hated Delhi. Not the city but its men. The way they looked at her, the way they spoke to her, the way they didn't speak to her, the personal space they invaded as if it was their birthright. She'd wanted to slap the entitlement plastered across their stupid faces. In her office, two men harassed her by cracking inappropriate jokes or passing suggestive comments. Another hounded her online with hundreds of messages like 'Hi, Hello, Hey, Whassup, Good morning, How are you?' while avoiding her in person. When she spoke to HR, no action was taken. She worried that senior management might call her up and threaten to let her go for being a troublemaker. So much fear and tension. But no, in Mama's eyes, Anu's move to Delhi was one of magic, of the laws of physics rewritten to suit her whims.

Something warm splattered against her wrist. Mama was weeping, gasping for air as food fell from her mouth. 'Oh,' she groaned, 'how could this happen?' Poppy rose to console her. 'What did I do to deserve this? Why am I being punished, for what reason?'

She's gone, Jyoti wanted to scream. And not because of any great reason but because some idiot drank too much and crashed into their car.

'You... you're getting food on the bed, Mama.'

'I feel so hollow.' Mama's hands grasped hers. 'Like I have no organs. Just skin. Just bones.'

'Eat your dinner. It'll help. Then you can rest. Come on.'

Like an obedient child, Mama spooned rice into her mouth, mumbling and crying to herself. When she was done, she was trembling. 'I'm cold.'

'Drink some water.'

There was a knock on the door and Varun spoke. 'Jyoti Aunty?'

'Yes?'

'When are we eating?'

Before she could reply, Mama clattered her spoon against the plate and pushed it hard against her arm. 'Take it away!' she said. 'Take it away and leave me be. I want to rest.'

'Fine, fine.'

'Go. And take the boy.'

Jyoti accepted both plate and dismissal. 'Come,' she said to Varun. 'Your grandmother needs to rest. She's had such an exhausting day lying in bed doing nothing.' Before Mama could respond, she shut the door.

9

After the lights in the house had been switched off and everyone had gone to sleep, Usha climbed out of bed. The hem of her nightie rustled against her ankles as she checked first on Varun and then on Jyoti. She always expected Jyoti to catch her, to lift her head from her pillow and call out, 'Mama, is that you?'

But no, Jyoti inhaled and exhaled softly into her pillow.

The shelves of Jyoti's room were cluttered with clay figurines, bowls, and glazed vases that shone in the dark. Some made by Jyoti, some by her students. How long had it been since Jyoti visited the art studio? She and that Tara girl had made plans to use a kiln. Ever since Anu's death, Jyoti's personal life had dissolved, like mud washed away by water. But that was true for all three of them.

'Sleep, little queen,' she whispered.

Usha checked the stove, the iron, the windows, and the door locks. In the living room, she noticed a book was missing from her husband's collection. What had Varun borrowed? She investigated and found the hardback on his desk. It was an encyclopaedia of wildlife in Bangalore, outdated of course, and bookmarked on a page with labelled illustrations of black kites in flight. Why was he reading this? Did he want to draw them? She remembered Anu telling her about an art project he'd spent weeks working on, borrowing books from the library to research Indian wildlife and learn their Latin names. His final painting had been awarded a silver star. And now? The poor boy, now he wasn't drawing or painting at all.

She ran her fingers across the glossy pages. How many years had this book stood on the shelf? Not once had she opened it.

She returned to her bedroom, shut the door, and switched on the television. The glare from the screen filled the room with a soft blue light. Poppy's eyes reflected the light. Usha sat on the toilet and urinated. She crawled back under the covers, and Poppy pawed at her hand till she scratched her ears.

In front of her, muted scenes from a film unfolded. The corner of the screen was cracked, bleeding light in pixelated streaks. The crack was from when her frustration had got the better of her and not, as she had told Jyoti, from low blood pressure causing her to stumble.

Broken television. Busted generator. Leaking bathroom. Warped window frames. Paint flaking from the walls. Silverfish crawling everywhere.

Usha sighed. Her lower back throbbed. She was exhausted, and though she knew she'd have to wake up at a reasonable time to have tea with Esther, she wished she could stay like this, in the dark, watching images flicker across a cracked screen.

Let the world figure out the rest.

10

The first thing Varun thought of when he woke up was that he'd brought something with him from the place beyond the wall. He leapt out of bed and looked for his shorts, but they weren't in the room. Jyoti Aunty must've put them away after he fell asleep.

He eased open his bedroom door and stepped out. No one else was awake. From where he stood in the hallway, he could see Jyoti Aunty curled up in bed. She was clutching the blanket. Beside her pillow lay her phone. He'd heard her talking last night to that uncle called Praveen. Grandma's bedroom door was shut.

It was early, and though he needed to be quick, he paused in the living room to pick up the landline and gently dial one of the few numbers he knew by heart. The phone rang on the other end six times before a sleepy voice answered, 'Hello?'

He gripped the phone.

'Yes? Hello?' said the voice. 'Can you hear me?'

He could see aunty opening the door for him, letting him in, and calling Komal from her bedroom. Sometimes aunty and Ma sat down together for tea, cracking jokes about the old uncles in the colony.

'Who is this? Why do you keep calling this number? Please stop. Look at the time! I'm going to report you, just you wait.'

He hung up. Chest tight with memories of Munirka, he stumbled into the kitchen and rummaged through the laundry basket, digging through fistfuls of damp clothes that carried an unpleasant smell of mushrooms. His shorts were tangled up in Grandma's enormous moth-eaten underwear. Wrinkling his nose, he pulled the two apart. He slid his hand inside the right pocket of his shorts. Nothing. He double-checked. Nothing. He slid his hand inside the left pocket of his shorts and, yes, there was something! He wrapped his fingers around the rough edges of the coin.

He crept back to his room and dived under the blanket to inspect his treasure. If only Pa was here, he'd be able to explain the coin. He had an album that contained coins of different shapes and sizes. *They're important, beta, they mean something. Look at the engravings. Each one is a token by which we can remember events in Indian history.* On this coin there was an engraving of Mahatma Gandhi with a staff, leading a crowd of people. Printed beneath the image were the words:

1947–1997
स्वतंत्रता का 50 वाँ वर्ष : *50th YEAR OF INDEPENDENCE*

On the other side was the number '50' with the words:

भारत *INDIA*
सत्यमेव जयते
पैसे *50 PAISE*

Varun recognized the state emblem of India, the Lion Capital of Ashoka. Pa had explained how it had four lions on a circular pedestal, their backs to one another. They represented confidence, courage, power, and pride. But only three lions were visible.

The fourth one sits behind the central lion. It's hidden from view.

There was a purple stain on the coin, similar in colour and shape to the birthmark on Pa's forearm. Like someone had spilt ink over his skin. Varun traced the stain. He put the coin in his mouth and concentrated on its metallic taste, its edges clinking against his teeth. He knew that place, hidden from view, was strange with its silence and the voice from the shadows. But there was the pool. And this coin.

Look, the voice had said.

What if he did look again? What else was waiting to be found?

11

The water pressure was low and the shower dribbled, coughed and sputtered. Usha leaned against the wall. Her legs ached, her back ached, and her eyes were gritty from lack of sleep. If only Esther was coming in the afternoon, but no, it was always after church service, invigorated by faith and a desire for gossip. She got dressed and combed her hair, only then noticing that her roots were showing silver. The framed photograph of her husband hung askew over the doorway, his thick bifocals reflecting the light of the camera, the edges of his lips pulled upwards in a smile.

In the living room, she found Jyoti dressed in a crisp blue sari with her hair tied up in a neat bun. Varun was wearing a clean shirt tucked into pressed trousers.

'Are you ready?' Jyoti asked.

'For what?'

'To go. We're going to be late if we don't leave soon.'

'Go where? Esther is coming over for tea.'

'We're supposed to see the lawyer today, don't you remember?'

'I can't come.'

'What? Why?'

'I told you, no?'

'Because of Mrs Naronha? Just cancel. She'll understand.'

'It's too late. It would be rude.'

'Mama, what are you saying? You can't keep missing these meetings. The lawyer specifically said that we both need to attend them. I told you about this last week, for heaven's sake.'

'What am I supposed to tell Esther? I'll come next time.'

Jyoti rubbed her forehead. She looked exactly like her father. They were both so alike, unable to mask their anger. Both of them would go for long walks together, leaving Usha alone in the house while they conspired.

'Mama, this is ridiculous.'

'Just go without me.'

'But–'

'You yourself said you were running late.'

Looking as though she was ready to snap her cane in half, Jyoti took Varun's hand and led him out of the house. They walked down the driveway, pausing briefly to greet Esther. Usha stood by the door, waiting. The sooner she and Esther exchanged inanities and swallowed down their teas, the better. She massaged her wrists to still the tremor in her hands.

'Hello, dear, how are you doing?' Esther called out.

'Oh, you know me.'

Esther came close and touched her arm in greeting. She smelled of perfume. Her thinning hair was hennaed orange and she wore rouge and a mauve lipstick that did nothing but highlight her age. 'Holding up okay?' she asked.

Usha looked beyond Esther, to the end of the driveway where her daughter and grandson were trying to hail an auto. 'Of course. I'm perfectly fine.'

12

They were stuck in traffic and Jyoti Aunty kept muttering to herself about Grandma and how late they were. Varun watched a family of three on a motorbike. The father at the front, the mother at the back, and in-between them a girl of his age. She smiled at him and he waved, curling his toes in his shoes and blushing. The father saw a break in traffic and signalled left, sticking his hand out to indicate where he wanted to go. The girl copied him. Together, the family wove through the gridlock and out of sight.

Jyoti Aunty was frantic by the time they reached. 'Quickly!' she said, paying the auto driver and bundling Varun out. Circles of perspiration darkened the underarms of her blouse. She tapped her phone, listened to the automated voice read out directions, and led him towards a building they'd visited before. People walking on the pavement either stared at Jyoti Aunty sweeping her cane in front of her or avoided them as though afraid of contamination. They hurried to the offices of L. H. Legal Associates, where Jyoti Aunty told the receptionist the name of the lawyer they were there to meet.

'He's with a client, ma'am. Please sit.'

'Any idea how long he'll be?' Jyoti Aunty asked.

'He'll be with you shortly.'

They waited an eternity.

And their meeting lasted less than five minutes. During those five minutes, the lawyer gestured at Varun several times, emphasized the words 'male guardian', and discussed husbands, fathers, grandfathers, uncles, or any male relatives in the family who were possibly still alive. 'It would help,' he said. 'Otherwise, there will be a lot more questions.'

Jyoti Aunty shook her head.

'Okay, I'll be in touch,' the lawyer said.

They were ushered out by the receptionist, who held the door open for them. Strands of hair had twisted loose from Jyoti Aunty's bun, and her upper lip was dotted with perspiration.

'Is it over?' he asked her.

'I have no idea. No. But for today, yes.'

How could there be three answers to the same question? 'I don't understand what happened.'

'Same.' She chuckled. 'This stuff is complicated. And I wish your grandmother would help. But thank you for being so patient. How are you? Tired?'

'Hungry. Can we go back?'

She listened to her phone. 'We're supposed to go to the tailor to pick up your school uniform, but it's quite late. What do you think? Chuck it?'

'Chuck it.'

'Okay. Why don't we eat out? Chicken tikka? You like that, don't you?'

'Yeah! How'd you know?'

She took his hand. 'Your mother told me it was your favourite. Apparently, the first time you tried it, you ate so much that they were scared you were going to be sick.'

'Really?'

'You kept asking for more, and nearly cried when you were told no. And even though your father told you not to do it, you licked the plate clean. Anu found it hilarious.'

'I didn't know that.'

'What's wrong?'

'Nothing.' But Varun was wondering what else Ma had told Jyoti Aunty about him. And what else Jyoti Aunty knew about Ma. He could ask. There was no harm in asking. Instead, he allowed himself to be led by Jyoti Aunty to a nearby restaurant. When she looked over the menu card and asked what he wanted, he remembered how Pa would ask, *What do you want, Anu?* and Ma would tease him by saying, *Only you, no?*

They returned to the bungalow at around three in the afternoon.

'Can I go play?' he asked.

'Hmm... I don't know. Don't you have homework to do?'

'But we were inside that office for so long!'

'What about the boxes we have to unpack?'

'This evening?'

'Promise?'

'God promise.'

'Fine. But change first. I don't want you ruining your nice clothes. And my friend is coming over later, Aunty Zarina, remember her? Make sure you say hello to her, okay?'

'Okay, Jyoti Aunty! Thanks, bye!'

He changed and ran into the grove. The rains had turned the ground to sludge and twice he slipped. His shoes were filthy by the time he caught sight of the bougainvillea and the hole in the boundary wall. The sounds of construction were ear-splitting. He remembered the fear in Poppy's eyes, the strange voice, and how it had tried to grab at his legs.

He toed the ground. What he needed was protection. He spotted the same stick he'd used yesterday as a cane and picked it up. Though damp, it was reassuringly heavy. He swished it through the air and imagined thrashing shadowy attackers.

In his pocket was the coin. Pa would flick the coin into the pool and, after counting five seconds, would ask *Ready?* before diving into the water with a laugh.

'Ready.'

Squeezing the stick in one hand, the coin in the other, Varun clambered through the hole in the wall. Once he was through, the shattered bricks rebuilt themselves, filling up the empty space so that within seconds the wall was whole. Varun had once again crossed over.

13

Poppy lay on the carpet listening to her sister and her ma argue.

'I can't believe you didn't come with us.'

'Next time.'

'That's what you said the last time! You can't keep doing this, Mama.'

'It's over, why're you giving me this lecture?'

'And now you're back in bed.'

'I'm tired, Jyoti. Unlike you, I didn't sleep very well. Try to be a little bit considerate. I had to listen to Esther go on and on about how the storms have disconnected her phoneline and flooded her parking lot.'

'Oh yes, how difficult it must be to sit at home and sip tea while we stew in a lawyer's office.' Her sister clattered out of the room. She always bumped into things when she was angry. Poppy followed after her to console her, but she locked herself in her bedroom and turned up the volume of her radio. Poppy pawed the bottom of the door till her claws shredded wood. No response.

There was a draft coming from the kitchen. She investigated and found the door to the back garden unlocked and ajar. Outside, the rains had washed away territory lines. She took pleasure in sniffing mulch and marking trees. A hearty smell of pressed clothes and hot charcoal came from the stall down the road. She wished the man who delivered bread would visit. The large steel box strapped to the back of his bicycle contained such delicious aromas. She enjoyed his visits because, no matter what, her ma would grumble about prices or the quality of the food from the bakery dropping over the years. There was nothing as reassuring as hearing her ma complain.

Searching for a stick to play fetch with, she realized that the boy was nowhere in sight. Her tail stiffened. She checked the grove and caught a sharp scent, like that of muscles tensed to spring into action.

Inquisitiveness.

The tunnel had called out and he'd gone answering. She thought he had more sense than that! Why were boys so interested in testing their limits? What was this great desire to steal back and forth across boundaries?

Poppy sat down at the edge of the grove. Her ma needed comforting and her sister needed support. And here was the boy, no longer trailing rancid bitterness but something just as bad. Poppy knew what such a feline scent meant. A boy's inquisitiveness led to mischief. A boy's mischief led to trouble. And the last thing they needed right now was trouble.

But it wasn't the boy's fault. Not entirely. During her time as a stray, she'd heard stories of tunnels luring people away from their homes, swallowing them up in the darkness of the earth.

It was difficult. She didn't like to show it, but it was difficult to suppress fear and pretend to be brave in the face of danger. Though she barked at stray dogs nosing at the gate, she meant them no ill will. She knew the trials they went through and could see the terror etched into their faces. Sometimes all she wanted was to lick clean their paws and offer them refuge.

Ignoring the aches in her joints, she rose and followed the trail of inquisitiveness. She winced when she heard the tunnel's hiss and crackle. Hopefully, there was still time. Hopefully, the boy hadn't gone through.

14

Varun watched the hole smooth itself out of existence. His hand trembled as he brushed the wall's surface and came away with dusty fingertips. Where had it gone? And why? There was no turning back now, but this was definitely a problem. He used the edge of the coin to mark an 'x'. At least he knew where to look, and if the hole didn't reappear then he would just have to climb over the wall and not cut himself on the shards of glass. There was nothing else he could do but carry on.

The courtyard was silent. There was the drained swimming pool, the pavilion with its broken pillar. He watched the shadows, but nothing moved. Did he really want to tempt fate? He took the coin out of his pocket, flipped it, and whispered, 'Heads, I go. Tails, I go back.' He imagined Pa doing the same, flipping the coin into the pool, and even before he plucked the coin from mid-air, he knew what he was going to do. Still, he glanced at fate's advice.

Tails.

Gripping the stick, he edged his way forward. There were plenty of loose tiles and broken stones, and the last thing he wanted was to make a loud sound or twist his ankle. Maybe in school it was good to be a 'wounded warrior', but not here. In all the fables he'd read in his old library, or the adventure books he and Pa read before bed, there was often a band of heroes who embarked on a quest. He was alone. But he was carrying a stick and a coin. 'Ready?' he whispered.

Yes, said the coin. *Do not fear.*

We're with you, said the stick.

Drawing courage from their words, he walked past the pool and out of the courtyard. There was a road. Across the road was a colony of crumbling houses. Some of the houses had collapsed, spilling rubble everywhere. Those houses that were still standing were bleached of colour, water-stained, their windows so scratched and dusty that they looked like cloudy eyes. He shivered at the thought of stepping inside their unlit rooms.

Not that way.

Safer to follow the road.

Varun agreed with his companions. And anyway, Ma hadn't yet given him permission to cross roads by himself.

But home is not here. Not in this place. The rules are different.

Home is in another city where the courtyard's clean and there's water in the swimming pool.

'Okay, okay.' His companions spoke in the same paired way as his parents did when they lectured him. It was both sweet and annoying.

They crept along the side of the road, which was in terrible condition. There were many potholes, some as deep as Varun's body. His stomach twisted as he imagined a car driving into one of them.

'Is this a mistake?'

We'll be careful.

The first sign of trouble and we'll hurry back.

They were approaching a park. The fence, made of iron

bars, was so warped that it had shattered its base and fallen to the ground. He tried to lift it, but it was impossibly heavy. Like the courtyard, the park was abandoned. He stepped off the stone pavement and on to hard earth that had caked and split. Grass crackled under his feet. The trees were leafless. Their branches were bone-thin and knotted. Many had been uprooted, wrenched from the earth with their blackened roots outstretched like hundreds of hands grasping at the sky.

Varun squeezed the coin. 'Isn't this a sign of trouble?'

Well, maybe.

But those look familiar.

In one corner of the park were the remains of playground equipment. The collapsed frame of a slide. The broken plastic seats of a swing. He remembered swooping through the air, the green of the park blurring as he picked up speed while Ma shouted at him to be careful. Alongside the playground was a walking path.

He followed the path, which looped around the park and between the trees. In the mornings, women with long-handled brooms swept the trail, swirling dust into the air while aunties who were walking coughed irritably or wrapped their faces with shawls. It was the same path, it had to be! And in the middle of the park was a rectangular patch of flattened ground. It was the batting pitch where they played cricket. By the entrance was a rusty metal box where a boy from a nearby store sold bread, eggs, and paper cups of chocolate milk. He spun on the spot and whooped. Here he was, standing in the same park as the one in his colony, the same park where he would guess the names of trees with Ma!

Or fly kites with Pa.

'Yes!'

Or play badminton with Komal.

'Yes!'

He ran further down the path to the stone bench where he and Ma fed biscuits to stray dogs. He'd named his favourites Timmy, Buster, Mel, and Scooty, but everyone in the colony had their own set of names for the dogs. Most of the aunties simply called them Brownie.

He sat on the bench. It was gritty and cool. His feet didn't reach the ground. Before, clusters of nasturtiums grew around the bench, their beautiful leaves open like saucers and brushing against his shins. It had taken him a very long time to learn the plant's name. He'd remembered only after their fiery orange flowers bloomed.

Varun looked at the trees. They were no longer recognizable. There used to be Amaltas, Imli, Neem, and a beautiful Peepal. Ma liked to sit on this bench and ask him to guess their names. But he'd begun to resist, especially when he could play badminton with Komal or join the older boys hammering wickets into the ground and calling for a game of cricket. He'd once screamed at her, 'No!' when she called him back. Why? Why hadn't he stayed with her?

Because you were bad.

Because you were ungrateful.

He picked at a scab on his elbow till a bead of blood rolled down his arm.

There was no breeze. The trees lay perfectly still. Why were they like that? What had happened here, and what about–

Shush.

What's that?

Varun listened. There was an electric hum in the air, like a motor whirring to life after being connected to a battery. The light in the park dimmed as the sun slipped behind clouds. He glanced around, half-expecting the world to transform and the dead trees to sink their roots back into the ground and tower over him.

He shivered. Maybe it was time to go back?

Yes.

Definitely.

Clenching the stick so tight that his palms ached, he stood up. His shoes scraped grit and he tensed at the sound, and it was in that moment that he heard the voice whisper again, Look.

Varun leapt.

There was no one behind him but he took off, sprinting out of the park and down the road back to the courtyard. Air whooshed around him and the soles of his feet ached as he ran as hard as he could.

He reached the wall and thumped the spot marked 'x'. The hole didn't reappear. Sweat trickled down his forehead and burnt the corners of his eyes. 'Come on!' There was no time for this! He kicked and shouldered the spot, but nothing happened. There was nothing else to do, he would just have to climb over the wall.

Look, said the voice again.

'No,' Varun yelped. The courtyard was empty. He didn't know who was speaking or where the voice was coming from, but he didn't want to be here anymore, didn't want to be trapped in this strange place with this strange voice.

Don't you know where you are?

He wanted to go back.

Can't you tell?

He wanted to go back to the bungalow and Jyoti Aunty and Grandma. As though it heard what he was thinking, the wall cracked open. Bricks turned to powder and the hole formed and expanded in front of his eyes.

No. Wait.

Varun slid a leg through the hole.

Stay.

He glanced behind him. The courtyard was still empty. But there was movement now. The flicker of a shadow in the ruins of the pavilion.

Varun, where are you going?

He fell through the hole, scraping his knee. On the other side came the roar of construction as clouds of dust heaved over the wall. He scrambled to his feet. He dropped the stick and ran. He raced back to the bungalow, ripping through bushes and leaping over puddles.

Varun, the voice had called out. The voice knew his name.

15

Poppy dreamt of home. Not where she lived with her ma and sister but the place where she'd been born. She could only recall a few images. Her mother's long snout, huddling with her siblings for warmth, learning each other's smells, and suckling milk.

Then the man arrived. He had separated them from their mother, beating her whenever she snarled or resisted. Some of her siblings were given to men and women in exchange for scraps of paper. This had continued for days. Then he returned for the last of them.

Poppy kicked. She was in a dream and wanted to wake up. Not there. She never wanted to be back there again. She thrashed against the muddy ground and experienced a shock to the senses as the world rushed into being around her. There were the sounds of construction, birds flapping away, and the pounding of footsteps as someone ran past her towards the house.

Disoriented, she nibbled on blades of grass. Her strength returned. She remembered that she was in the grove, following the boy's scent towards the hiss and crackle of the tunnel. But something had happened. She'd been stopped in her tracks by memories so terrible and vivid that she could almost feel the man's rough hands grabbing her by the scruff of her neck.

She trembled.

She had no idea how much time had passed since she set out, but the sun was now low in the sky. And where was the boy? She crept forward, tail tucked between her legs and her body hugging the ground.

Ahead of her, the air began to ripple. There were distortions and she stared at the branches of a tree as they warped into a spiral. What had the boy done? Summoning all of her courage, she peered around a tree trunk.

The vertical line of darkness continued to hiss and crackle, but it had deepened, widened. It was as though some force had strained at the fabric of this world and ripped it apart at the seam. The edges of the vertical line fluttered. There was space. Poppy backed away with a whine. There was space now for things to come through.

16

Jyoti answered the door and was nudged out of the way by Zarina, who went straight to the kitchen. Jyoti followed after her.

'Hi,' Zarina said, hefting something heavy on to the kitchen counter and then sweeping her into a back-breaking hug.

'Can't. Breathe.'

'Don't be so dramatic. I made you berry pulao.'

'Yes! I haven't had that in ages.'

'You told me.'

'Thank you,' Jyoti said, extricating herself from the hug. She cracked open the lid of the tiffin box to inhale the aromatic scents of rice cooked in saffron and ghee, and a mutton curry rich in ginger and garlic. Her mouth watered. She was still full from lunch with Varun, but she couldn't resist helping herself to a heaped spoonful.

Zarina laughed. 'Any good?'

'If you don't take it away from me right now, I'll hundred percent polish it off.'

'Good. You need to eat. You're like a toothpick.'

Jyoti couldn't respond because her mouth was full.

'Here, give me that,' Zarina said. She sealed the tiffin box and slid it inside the fridge, then clattered about the kitchen, igniting the stove, and pouring water into a vessel before rummaging through the cupboards. Occasionally she knocked over things on the counter and berated Jyoti. 'How can anyone cook in here? It's like a bloody cupboard.'

Jyoti smiled. She didn't mind the cramped space of the kitchen. Just a few days ago, she'd made a snack for Praveen when he'd come visiting. He'd tried to help but only got in the way, and twice their bodies had brushed against each other.

'Tea's ready,' Zarina said. 'You okay? You're looking all hot and bothered.'

'I'm fine. Come on.'

Arms interlinked, they stepped outside with their cups of tea and strolled down the driveway. A crisp breeze ruffled their clothes.

'How're the children?' Jyoti asked.

'Noisy. Wretched things. Fifth Standard are learning to play cricket in PE and the only thing I could hear all afternoon was the rattle of that bloody cricket ball. I should complain. Maybe Hema can give them a good beating.'

'Very funny.'

'Who's joking? Even with my headphones on I couldn't concentrate. Who's the genius who decided to put the computer department right next to the playground?'

Jyoti chuckled.

'Rukmini keeps asking me when you'll return. She's desperate to show you her newest clay creation.'

'I can't wait. Soon.'

'That's what I told her. She was very excited.'

'Sweet girl.'

'So, you're sticking with the plan and coming back to work on Monday?'

'Why not?'

'Just asking.'

'Yes, I'm back on Monday.'

'Okay.'

'I've used up all my leave, so I have to come back to work. I don't have a choice.'

'Okay, okay, no need to bite my head off.'

They walked in silence to the gate, turned around, and headed back to the house. Jyoti chucked the rest of her tea in the bushes.

Zarina pulled her close. 'Tell me.'

'Nothing.'

Zarina clicked her tongue. 'Something's bugging you. Don't be so pricy. Just tell me. Was the meeting with the lawyer a mess?'

'Massive mess. Anu and Alok left no will. Obviously. Who makes a will at their age? Have you made one? I don't have one.' Jyoti rubbed her forehead. 'This whole process is complicated. And my mother isn't helping. And there's the usual problem.'

'What's the usual problem?'

'We need a man, a heroic male guardian.'

'Ah.'

'No husband? No father? No male relative? And blind? Who will provide for us and who do we list as the head of the household?'

'Time to get married.'

'Yes. Of course. I'll go ask one of my hundreds of boyfriends to propose. This same stupid issue came up when I was hunting for a school for Varun. One of them insisted that we provide the child's father's income certificates. Otherwise, tough luck.'

Zarina clicked her tongue. 'A man's certificate.'

'This all reminds me of when my mother was obsessed with getting me married. Like I was on the verge of becoming expired goods. I tell you, I'm sick of the word dependent.'

Zarina folded her into a hug and rubbed her back.

'Sorry. I'm tired and cranky today,' Jyoti said.

'No need to apologize.'

'There's just so much to do. I still haven't finished the grant application and the deadline is coming up soon. What will Hema say? I don't-'

'Shh, shh, shh.'

Jyoti stopped talking and allowed herself to be held by Zarina.

'Don't worry, I'll help you with all that rubbish. Now take a deep breath.'

She inhaled.

'And let it out.'

She exhaled in a whoosh.

'Again.'

She inhaled and exhaled again.

'Okay?'

'Okay.'

'See? Better now. No need to keep it all bottled up.'

They returned to the house to drop off their empty cups before looping around the back garden. Jyoti's head was once again filling up with all the millions of things she had to do when she heard twigs snapping, huffing and puffing, and footsteps skidding to a halt.

'Your child has just emerged from the trees,' Zarina whispered. 'It looks like he went swimming in mud.'

'Again?'

Zarina laughed.

'Anu never told me that having a child means having to deal with a mountain of laundry every single day.'

'He also looks very guilty. Definitely been up to no good.'

'Varun, come say hi, no?' Jyoti said, remembering the times when Mama would ask her and Anu to do the same if there was a guest.

'Hi, aunty,' Varun mumbled.

'Hello, child,' Zarina said cheerfully. 'Tell us what business you've been up to.'

'Nothing.'

'Who knew doing nothing could be so messy? Did you read that book I gave you? On cats?'

'Not yet.'

'Not yet? And why not? I'm telling you, you'll love it.'

'I'm in the middle of another book.'

'Which book?' Zarina demanded.

Jyoti spared Varun the misery of further interrogation. 'There are some slices of apple in the fridge. Go wash up and eat. Make sure you use soap.'

'Okay, Jyoti Aunty.'

She heard him kick off his shoes by the back door and step inside the house.

'He's hurt himself,' Zarina said. 'His left knee is bleeding. No need to panic though. It's just a scrape.'

'I don't know what he's up to.'

'Probably climbing trees and falling flat on his face.'

'Shush! Don't say such things.'

'Oh please, he's a boy, that's what they do. Listen, I have to go, I don't want to get stuck in traffic. Call me if you need anything, okay? I can make you some cutlets if you like.' Zarina kissed her on the cheek and left.

Inside, Jyoti retrieved the medicine kit and waited for Varun. He brought with him a clean scent of soap. She instructed him to sit down in the living room, twisted open the bottle of antiseptic, and sloshed a generous amount into a ball of cotton gauze. She found his right knee, then his left knee.

'This will sting.'

She wiped his knee and he gasped. His smooth skin had been scraped raw. The poor thing. She winced as he clenched his little legs.

'How did you hurt yourself like this?'

'I fell.'

'Fell where?' For an instant she imagined him plummeting from the top of a tree.

'By the driveway? I tripped.'

He wasn't very good at lying. Which was a surprise. At his age, she and Anu had already developed their own secret language for times when Mama was in a vindictive mood. Though, of course, their secret language only further infuriated Mama. She bandaged his knee. 'There. Better?'

'Does anyone else live here, Jyoti Aunty?'

'Meaning?'

'Meaning, is there someone here? Someone with a strange voice?'

'A strange voice? What do you mean? Did you see someone here?'

'No.'

'Varun. Did you see someone here?'

'No, no.'

'Are you talking about Seema's husband? Rakesh? He takes care of the garden once a week.'

'No, Jyoti Aunty, never mind, it's okay.'

Jyoti thought hard about the people who visited the house. There were quite a few of them. 'The dhobi? The man who brings bread on Wednesday and Friday mornings? The milkman? Or what about the newspaper delivery man? Are you talking about any of them?'

'No, I made a mistake, there was nobody.'

But then why on earth would he ask such a question?

'Can I go?' he asked.

'Wait,' she said. 'Are you opening the gate and going out? Are you going down the road to maybe play with those children in the apartment complex? Don't be afraid, you won't be in trouble, but I need to know.'

'No, Jyoti Aunty. I'm not. Please can I go now?' He didn't wait for her permission and hurried off to his bedroom.

Jyoti sank into a chair. Someone with a strange voice? Who could that possibly be? Was Varun wandering up and down the road, maybe to find a store to buy sweets for himself? Some money had gone missing recently. Ten rupees here, twenty rupees there. She didn't want to believe he might be stealing, but maybe that's what was happening.

If only Mama would help.

The doorbell rang.

'Jyoti,' Mama called out sleepily. 'Someone at the door.'

'Really? I had no idea,' she said to herself. She went to answer the door.

'Jyoti?' Mama called out again.

She ignored her. It felt good to ignore Mama. The doorbell rang again just as she yanked the door open. 'Yes? Who is it?

What do you want and why are you ringing the bell so many times?'

'Hmm,' said a rough voice, 'it sounds like I've caught you at a bad time.'

'Oh.' Jyoti tried to compose herself. 'Hi, Praveen.'

17

Usha could hear a man's voice coming from the living room. She eased open her bedroom door to investigate. It was the Rao's boy, Praveen. Visiting for the second time in ten days. He used to be such a gangly child with braces and wisps of hair curling over his upper lip. Now he was tall and lean with a deep voice, sitting on the divan next to Jyoti and booming with laughter.

She changed into something more presentable, cleaned the sticky yellow dirt from the corners of her eyes, then walked past the living room and pretended to only just notice him.

'Good evening, aunty,' he said, rising.

'Sit, sit. Nice to see you again, beta. How're your parents?'

'They're fine, thank you. My mother told me to tell you, if you need anything, anything at all, please don't hesitate to call us. We're always here for you.'

'Oh, she's very kind.'

'You both should come over for dinner.'

'We will, won't we, Jyoti?'

Jyoti grunted. So uncouth. She should oil her hair. It looked dull and lifeless.

'And how are you, aunty?'

'Fine, fine, all well.' She ignored the face Jyoti was making. 'I'll leave you both to chit chat. I have to go make dinner now.' Before Jyoti could pass some snide remark, she smiled at Praveen and went to the kitchen, where she pretended to cook but mostly stood at the stove and listened to the two of them. They were reminiscing about school and the mischief Praveen got into. This was what they did now, talk about the past. She supposed it was a kind of refuge.

He used to come over after school and play with the girls when they were children, but somewhere along the way he stopped visiting. Maybe it became an inconvenience or maybe the Raos thought it inappropriate after Jyoti lost her sight. Other families certainly alienated them. Residents on the street learnt to ignore them when they crossed paths, self-consciously avoiding eye contact. Or worse, pretending to care by talking down to Jyoti like she was some sort of simpleton.

She heard Jyoti ask him about work and struggled to stifle a groan. The last time he'd gone on and on for hours about capital, freight forwarding, flat-packing goods, and meeting quality-control standards. The intricacies of a start-up. He spoke with such self-importance, despite his venture disastrously falling through. And the fact that his father had been the source of his funds. He'd exhausted his parents' patience and some six months ago they'd insisted he return to Bangalore from Bombay. Esther gossiped that in the evenings the family could be heard arguing.

And now here he was. Visiting so often.

Maybe he was interested in Jyoti. Would it be so bad if they got married? The family was snobbish, and he'd certainly made a mess of things in Bombay, but at least there would be someone to care for Jyoti in her old age. And financial security. Plus, he seemed to be a nice boy, harmless in his desire to please her.

'I miss Bombay,' he was saying. 'There's this four-kilometre stretch of Marine Drive between NCPA and Wilson College, which used to be my running circuit in the mornings. There's nothing like the sea. It makes the city feel so open, despite the muggy weather. Bangalore, on the other hand, is landlocked. And the traffic is hellish. I find it so claustrophobic.'

'I've never been to Bombay.'

'Should've visited me when you had the chance.'

'Oh yes?'

'I would've given you the grand tour. I'm sure you would've liked it.'

'Maybe,' Jyoti said. 'I understand what you mean about the claustrophobia. Bangalore can get stifling. Sometimes I think about going on a holiday to a nature reserve where it's quiet and peaceful. A brief escape from all this.'

Then go, Usha thought with vehemence. Go, and spare us your self-righteous martyrdom.

'Anu and I had been talking about going to Ranthambore. Just the two of us.'

Usha could hear no more. She banged pots and pans and tried to stifle the drone of their stupid conversation, but her head buzzed with the thought that her daughters had been planning a trip without her.

Someone's cell phone rang. Praveen said it was his father and excused himself.

Usha realized then that she hadn't heard Poppy bark when Praveen rang the doorbell. Nor had she seen the dog in some time. She opened the back door and whistled, but there was no sign of her. Where could she be? A blade of yellow light slanted across the hallway floor from the guest bedroom, its door open a crack, and she wondered if Varun was playing with Poppy. She tried to peer inside but could see little. She could, however, hear Varun making strange little sounds. Clicks and whooshes, a soft murmuring. They were familiar sounds from the recesses of her past when her daughters used to play with paper boats.

She nudged the door open an inch. The room was tidy except for an overturned chair on the carpet beside the bed. Varun sat folded in-between the legs of the chair with his hands meeting together to grip an invisible joystick. His eyes were narrowed in concentration. His body moved with the motions of the joystick, and it appeared as though he was diving. He had crafted a cockpit from a chair, an aeroplane from thin air, and perhaps right now was in the middle of a dogfight or streaking across the skies.

The door creaked.

Varun saw her and jumped. He scrambled to his feet and righted the chair as she knocked and let herself inside.

'Sorry, sorry,' she said.

His ears flushed pink and he stood behind the chair. He looked ready to spring away.

She sat on his bed. 'Were you flying a plane just now?'

'Submarine.'

'Oh, a submarine?' It was the opposite of what she'd imagined. Down instead of up. Ocean instead of sky.

Varun slid the chair under the desk. He climbed on to the bed and sat cross-legged on one end.

'You know, your mother and your aunt used to make paper boats of different shapes and sizes. So many of them! I don't know where they learnt to make them. Whenever it rained, they would run and find puddles and race each other with their boats. That or they would go exploring. They loved to do that. Your mother once told me they'd gone and explored an ancient civilization.'

He fidgeted with the stitches of his bed cover.

He was silent these days. There was a time when he would explode into rooms, tripping over carpets and demanding that everyone play hide-and-seek or fly kites with him. Anu had been so patient. But she'd raised him right. He was unlike all those other horrid children in the apartment complex who bossed around their maids or threw tantrums when they didn't get what they wanted. What if all of her daughter's parenting came undone?

She got up. She needed to be back in bed with the lights off and the television on. No more revelations about planned trips without her, no more thoughts about the responsibilities of parenthood.

'Grandma?'

'What?'

'Is it okay to go exploring?'

'Of course. Why ever not?'

'What if you get lost?'

'Lost? Where are you getting lost?'

'Never mind.'

'Tell me.'

'It's not like that.'

'Well… I used to worry about your mother and aunt when they went exploring. I always thought they were getting lost. But they were careful. And most of the time they were good. Not always, but most of the time.'

He smiled.

'So just be careful, okay?'

'Okay.'

'Good.'

She looked at his face, at his hair growing curly and wild. Her husband had nurtured Anu's passion for plants. When she was a child, Anu sometimes spent Sunday afternoons exploring the grove, crouching over plants or weeds and comparing them to illustrations in a book. When she returned, she tramped mud across the floors and filled the house with the smell of wet earth.

It was cruel that Varun behaved like his mother, yet looked so like his father.

'I think I'm going to rest, beta,' she said.

She hesitated. On his table was a model skeleton of a Tyrannosaurus Rex. A gift from Alok for his birthday. But none of his school drawings hung from the walls. None of his books lined the shelves. There was little to show that this was his room. Behind her, in the living room, she could hear Jyoti and Praveen gassing away like there was no tomorrow. She knew she should spend time with the boy, exchange warm memories of Anu and Alok with him, but she was tired.

'I'll shut the door if you want,' she said.

'Okay, Grandma.'

As she left, she saw him flip a coin.

18

Zarina's berry pulao was perfection. Varun asked for seconds, Mama couldn't fault it, and, alone in the kitchen, Jyoti licked clean her plate. She loosened her salwar's drawstrings. She wanted to collapse into bed and catch the news over the radio when she heard Poppy pawing the back door. 'And where have you been, madam?' she asked, letting her in. Poppy brushed past her shins. Her claws clicked against the stone floor as she crossed the hallway and nosed open a door to be greeted by a series of pleasant exclamations from Mama. Jyoti shook her head.

She went to check on Varun. 'Are you in bed?' she asked, knocking on his door.

'Yeah.'

A cool breeze flitted through his room. She sat on his bed and found he was already under the blanket.

'How's your knee? Does it hurt?'

'No.'

'Good. Make sure you keep the bandage dry. And you brushed your teeth?'

'Yeah.'

He sounded tired, the poor thing. She smoothed the blanket and tried to remember when she last had it washed.

And what about the mattress? It had been years since they dusted it in the sun.

'Jyoti Aunty?'

'Hmm?'

'Can I read tonight? Just for ten minutes?'

'What are you reading?'

He climbed out of bed. She heard him rummaging through the stuff on his desk before returning and placing a book on her thigh. She picked it up. The spine was cracked and rough against her thumb. It carried a wonderful smell of road-side bookstores.

'Where did you find this?'

'I didn't find it,' he said, a note of playfulness creeping into his voice. 'It's mine.'

'Then why is this the first time I'm hearing about it?'

'Because, Jyoti Aunty, it was in one of the boxes, which I unpacked all by myself before dinner, even though you were supposed to help me but you were too busy talking to that uncle!'

Jyoti smiled. 'My goodness! Well, that was very bad of me but very good of you.'

'I put away everything from one box. It's completely empty.'

'That's great. Thank you. So, what's the name of this book?'

He told her.

'What's it about?'

'You've never read it?' he asked, sitting up.

She tried not to laugh at his incredulity. 'It's good, then?'

'Good? Oh, Jyoti Aunty, it's so good, it's... it's the best story Pa and I have ever read in our entire lives! And we're only halfway through.'

'Wow. So... you both used to read this in the night?'

'Yeah.'

'And is this where you are right now?'

The book had opened to a page with its top corner folded in.

'Yeah.'

Tracing the fold, she realized it must have been some precious few weeks ago that Alok had stopped reading aloud to Varun and marked this page. This fold was a tangible memory of his past actions, which was a thought he would've highly approved of as a historian and cultural conservationist.

Varun lifted the book out of her hands. 'We're right now at the part with the black rabbit.'

'The black rabbit?'

'He's everlasting darkness.'

'What does that mean?'

She thought about losing her vision. She thought about nights spent weeping into her pillow till Anu consoled her. But Varun launched into an excited yet disordered summary of the book's characters and their journey to find a new home.

'You really need to read it, Jyoti Aunty! You... oh.' He went silent.

She traced his cheek. Such a sweet boy. 'I can read braille, but I don't think this book will be available in that format in India. I'll check. It sounds really interesting. You go ahead and read. But only for ten minutes, okay? Then bed.'

'Okay.'

'Night.'

'Is... is it hard to read braille?'

'It takes practice. I had a good teacher, but I used to get very impatient and cross. Some people can zoom across a page. Not me. There's a stencil in my bedroom with all of the letters, if you want to try it.'

'Okay. Goodnight, Jyoti Aunty.'

'Night.'

She made sure all the switches in the house were off and the windows and doors bolted shut. The living room still carried the scent of aftershave. Grinning like a fool, she made her way to her bedroom. It was nice of Praveen to visit. A distance had threatened to grow between them after Anu had passed, but he'd made all the effort to keep in touch. And despite his gruff exterior, he was so reassuring. He was right, children do scrape themselves while playing. They grow up learning to keep secrets. She and Anu had done the same. She recalled the day before she was going to start college when Anu had locked their bedroom door and given her a frank yet detailed lesson on sex, one that was more useful than any of the shame-filled, laughter-interrupted talks at school. The lesson did prompt her to ask about Anu's sources of information.

Jyoti chuckled.

She sent a message to Zarina, thanking her for the food, then fired up her laptop, and searched online for an audio version of the book Varun was reading. Thankfully, it existed. She paid for it, downloaded it to her phone, and clicked play.

The narrator spoke with a very British accent that reminded her of Papa's collection of leather-bound classics in the living room. The narrator read out the epigraph.

CHORUS: Why do you cry out thus, unless at some vision of horror?
CASSANDRA: The house reeks of death and dripping blood.
CHORUS: How so? 'Tis but the odour of the altar sacrifice.
CASSANDRA: The stench is like a breath from the tomb.

She paused it. What on earth was this? Surely it was too dark for Varun? She double-checked her purchase. It was the same book he was reading. And Alok had been reading it aloud to him, enjoying it with him, so obviously this had not been an issue. She tried to remember the books she'd been allowed to read at Varun's age, but could only recall stories by Enid Blyton, Roald Dahl, and other curiously British authors.

She clicked play, and though initially unsettled was soon lost in the world of the book, listening to chapter after chapter before realizing with a start that it was nearly midnight. Putting away her things, she thought about catching up to where Varun was in the book. Maybe he would like to listen to the audio version as well, and if not, they could always discuss the story. She crawled under her blanket and tried to sleep, her mind filled with images of bandages, books, and burrows.

19

Poppy lapped at the water in her bowl. She'd panted all evening, keeping watch as the vertical line crackled and hissed. But nothing had come through. Not yet. She lay on the threadbare carpet by the foot of her ma's bed and tried to rest, though the blood in her veins streaked like lightning.

She whined.

She sniffed the air.

She paced around in circles.

She whined again.

'Oh ho, what's the matter with you?' her ma asked.

Poppy drank some more water, but it did little to quell her nerves.

She nosed the carpet.

She crawled under the bed and lay with her stomach on the cool floor.

The bedframe creaked above her. Her ma's legs descended to the ground and her knee clicked as she crouched to peer at her. 'What's the matter?' Her annoyance was replaced by concern. 'Come on.' She extended her arms and dragged Poppy out. 'What's the matter, huh? Tell me,' her ma crooned, gently lifting her up on to the bed to inspect her paws.

Poppy licked her ma's palm. How to explain what was

happening? Her ma was so vulnerable right now. What if the tunnel was to lure her away? What if, one by one, those she loved most were taken away from this world? She let out a long high-pitched whine.

'Okay, okay. Come.' Her ma coaxed her under the blanket. The bed was soft, warm, and trapped within the mattress was the scent of lavender talcum powder. She remembered awful nights as a stray, shivering in drainpipes and gutters with the wind whipping her fur and monstrous glaring lights roaring at her. Where would she be if she hadn't found her ma's gate and the piles of chicken rice she left outside for strays? Her ma had rescued her. She buried her snout under her ma's legs. Her ma scratched the fur under her collar, stroked her back, and whispered soothing sounds. Slowly the tension in her body drained away and she slid into a deep sleep.

In her dreams, she kicked. There was the tunnel. The vertical seam of darkness was tearing itself open, its edges fluttering wider and wider, and from within a shadowy figure strained against the fabric of the world, desperate to cross over.

20

Varun and Jyoti Aunty were once again stuck in traffic, this time on their way to the tailor. He held a silent debate with himself as they waited. The place beyond the wall was clearly dangerous. First the voice, then the shadow in the ruins. And how did the voice know his name? But it had wanted him to stay there, to look. It had asked him if he knew where he was. And he did. Or he thought he did.

The blare of a bus horn snapped him out of his thoughts. By the side of the road lay a homeless man, his arm draped over his face. The clothes he wore were tattered, and Varun was struck by how exhaustion pinned him to the ground. Did the voice belong to a homeless person living inside those ruins?

He fidgeted with the coin in his pocket.

Characters in the story he was reading had faced a similar dilemma. To stay or go? Varun thought of the book, its worn cover and cracked spine. Pa loved a dog-eared book because it was proof that it was well read, maybe even well enjoyed. *Age doesn't rob an object of its beauty, beta. The opposite in fact.* It was how Pa felt about the heritage sites he worked so hard to protect. From baoli to baradari, there was much to learn from monuments, not just in terms of design but culture and history as well. *Our roots lie deep under their foundations. The answer to who we are as a people resides within their walls. How can we ignore them?*

Varun wished he could set off immediately for the place beyond the wall.

The auto driver steered them to the side of the road and stopped. Jyoti Aunty paid him. Her phone rang just as she was climbing out, and reaching for her bag to answer it, her shoulder bumped against the auto frame and she lost her balance. She fell. One of her wrists rolled over with a sickening pop.

'Jyoti Aunty!'

She sat hunched on the ground, clutching her wrist to her chest, and breathing hard with her eyes closed. At last, she whispered, 'I'm fine, don't worry.' She reached for her cane and stood up. Her forehead was pale, dotted with sweat, but she dusted the knees of her salwar as though nothing had happened.

All the while the auto driver remained in his seat, watching.

She made her way towards the tailor's. Varun didn't know if it was his imagination or not, but he thought she was moving slower than before. She reached out with an unsteady hand to clutch the railing leading up to the entrance of the shop, and his chest ached. Her palms were scraped.

She opened the door for him. 'Come on.'

Varun did as he was told. He tried on the clothes the tailor had prepared for him, but he was so distracted that he wore his shirt inside out.

'Do you need any help?' she asked from the other side of the door.

'I'm okay.'

He came out of the changing room in his new school uniform. She asked him how it felt while she traced the length and width of his clothes. She ran her fingers along the neckline of his shirt to check if it was too tight, tugged at the waistline of his trousers to make sure he could sit down comfortably, and when he sat down, she measured where the hemlines ended.

'How do you like the uniform?'

'It's nice,' he said, looking in the mirror at her swollen wrist.

'Is it smart? Or silly?'

'Smart.'

'Good.'

She paid the tailor and they left the store. He insisted on carrying everything.

'You're sure you can manage?'

'It's fine.'

'Okay. Now,' she said, dabbing at her forehead with her dupatta, 'what next?'

They went grocery shopping. He kept a watchful eye but she didn't trip or fall again. After buying groceries, they went to the post office. He tottered slightly from the weight of all the bags he insisted on carrying. When they were done, she hailed an auto and they were soon on their way back to the bungalow.

'Thanks for being so good,' she said.

'Does your hand hurt?'

'A little.'

'I'm sorry.'

'Why are you sorry? It was an accident. It's okay.'

'I should've helped.'

'Have you never fallen? Have you never hurt yourself?'

Varun didn't say anything.

'People trip and fall. It happens. There's no need to treat this as any different, okay?' She tried to rotate her wrist. 'Don't worry. I just need to ice it. It's no big deal.'

He leaned against her. He didn't want to know what she thought was a big deal.

21

Jyoti's wrist was sharp with pain by the time she turned the key in the lock and stepped inside the house. Varun followed after her, carrying all the bags. She headed straight for the freezer, and was surprised to find the kitchen empty.

'Seema?'

No response. No jingle of anklets.

She crushed ice in a cloth and wrapped it around her wrist. To distract herself from the pain, she went to check on Mama but very nearly tripped over the mountain of bags Varun had left by the kitchen door.

'Very nice,' she muttered to herself. 'First my wrist, then my neck.'

As a minor punishment, but mostly because she needed the help, she made Varun put away his clothes, unpack and store the groceries, and shell cloves of garlic.

'Jyoti?' Mama called out.

'Coming. What happened to Seema?'

'She called. Her husband is sick. Supposedly. A likely story. Have you noticed she always tries to skip Fridays?'

'Today's Thursday.'

'Same thing. I'm worried about Poppy. And what happened to your hand?'

'Did Seema say when she'll be back?'

'No. We should dock her pay.'

'Please, Mama, don't. The least we can do is help her, not punish her.'

'Why ever not? I have a good mind to. I'm not paying her to take holidays whenever she pleases. Did you fall?'

'I'm fine.' Water from the ice wrap dripped on to the floor. Seema's husband was old, and drank too much. The last time he was in the hospital for a liver problem, Seema hadn't turned up for two weeks. Maybe she should call and check on her. She should definitely make sure Mama didn't speak with her.

'You have to be more careful.'

'Yes, Mama.'

'I'm worried about Poppy.'

Jyoti turned away.

'Did you hear what I said? She's behaving very strangely.'

'Then take her to the vet. I don't have any time.'

'No time, no time,' Mama muttered.

She found Varun in the kitchen. He'd done as she had asked and now the poor thing reeked of garlic.

'Can I go play?' he asked.

'Where will you play?'

'Outside.'

The power died just then. Everything in the house rattled to a stop. Strange, considering it wasn't raining and there'd been no mention of load-shedding in the local news. The generator didn't even try to come to life. They really needed to get the damned thing fixed or replaced.

'Did the power go?' Mama called out. 'I forgot, those BESCOM people called and said there was an issue with our bill payment.'

'When did they call?'

There was no response.

'Mama. When did they call? Today? Or ages ago and you're only telling me now?'

Silence.

She sighed and let the ice wrap fall into the kitchen sink with a soggy thud. There was never a moment's rest in this house. And now she'd have to go to that blasted government office where inefficiency reigned.

'Jyoti Aunty?'

'Yes, Varun, yes, I heard you. Do you promise to be careful?'

'Promise.'

'No more hurts or scrapes?' she said, cradling her swollen wrist.

'God promise.'

'Then go.'

His footsteps were slow to the back door, which opened with a creak, and then he was scampering away from the house and into the grove. She was reminded of the time Anu wanted to build a treehouse but was forbidden by Mama. *Are you mad? You can't even keep your own room clean!* Undaunted, Anu had used tape and a shoebox to construct a small birdhouse. She'd even glued together twigs to form little chairs for the inside. A house within a shoebox. A shoebox that she taped to a slender tree in the grove. The cardboard turned soggy and disintegrated a week later in a storm, prompting Anu to ask Papa if he could teach her carpentry. Her sister, an engineer at such a young age.

From Mama's room came the click-click of a switch and a huff of annoyance.

'I'm leaving,' Jyoti said to the house, wishing she was on her way to Delhi and Anu.

22

Varun knelt by the bougainvillea and peered through the hole. The courtyard was empty and the shadows stretched long this late in the afternoon. He picked up the stick and climbed through the hole in the wall. The sounds of construction stopped. Silence enveloped him. Keeping his eyes on the pavilion, he tried to stay calm. There was a sliver of broken tile by his foot and he picked it up, ran his thumb across its curved edge, then hurled it into the shadows. It skittered across the courtyard. Nothing. No voice. No movement. But what did that mean? Jyoti Aunty had made him promise to be careful. Even Grandma had warned him to be careful.

Well? Is this being careful? asked the coin.

We could always go back, said the stick.

It was true, they could. The hole was still there. He frowned. Why was it still there? Every other time it had vanished after he'd crossed over. He took a step away, expecting the wall to rebuild itself, but it didn't.

What's different?

It makes no sense.

It didn't matter. What mattered was that they hurry and explore this place.

What do you mean?

Where are we going?
'The colony.'
What about the voice?
What about the shadow?
'We'll be careful.'
Don't you remember what happened?
How there was something in the ruins?
What if we get trapped in here?
Or lost?

'We won't. I know we won't.' Now that he was here, he knew he was right. And with that certainty came confidence. He walked around the empty swimming pool, past the ruins of the pavilion, and was just about to step out of the courtyard when he heard a crunch. He whirled around. But no, all was still, all was the same as before.

Except the hole in the wall was gone. Vanished at last.

He ignored the sounds of alarm from his companions, though his heart beat swiftly. Too late now. And anyway, he wanted to be here. This was his choice. He left the courtyard. After looking both ways, he crossed the road and inspected the entrance of the alley leading into the colony. Lying on the ground, half-buried by rubble, was a sign. It was so weather-beaten that it was difficult to read.

Impossible, said the coin.
It can't be, said the stick.

But it was. He wiped the signboard with the hem of his shirt and revealed two words: Munirka Enclave.

'I was right.'
But…
How?
'It's here.'

Wait.
Let's think about this.
'Think about what?'
It can't be Munirka Enclave.
The pool was never this close. The park wasn't down the road.
It makes no sense.
These places aren't where they should be.
It didn't matter. None of it mattered in comparison to what was ahead.

He clambered over the rubble and entered the alley. It was narrow and dimly lit by the fading sun. Shards of glass glinted from the shadows. His steps were light, gently placed, yet they echoed off the surrounding buildings. What if someone was in one of the buildings, watching him? Or worse, what if one of the buildings caved in and blocked his way back, trapping him here? What would he do then? He leapt over a broken drainpipe.

Something was wrong. He tried to stay calm but it was difficult. The house to his right should've been where the Sehgals lived. An army family, they had a flag of India that fluttered from their balcony railing. The uncle was a Sikh with a silver beard who wore turbans of bright colours. But there was no brightness here. Drain water had stained the walls in rings of black, and the roof of the top floor had collapsed.

Where are we?
Do you know?
'I... I think so.'
You think so?
You don't recognize this place?
'Maybe?'
Maybe?

Are we lost?

They couldn't be lost. He couldn't be wrong. He gazed at the collapsed roof. How many times had he and Komal snuck up to the terraces, despite their parents warning them not to, just so they could sit on the filthy sun-warmed rooftops and share cashew biscuits? She'd told him to call every day.

You can. You can call her today.

You can call her now. If we go back. Let's go back?

He thought of Komal, her eyes flashing as they made a pinky promise.

This time you can talk to her, tell her it's you who's been calling.

You don't have to be afraid.

She was kind to you.

She never let any of the other children bully you.

Remember how you promised to be best friends for life?

Remember how she hugged you the day after Ma and Pa-

'Stop,' he breathed.

Why don't we go back?

We don't have to stay in this place of shadows.

'Please stop.'

Varun nearly did turn back. But then he saw the telephone poles along the side of the alley. Black cables criss-crossed these telephone poles. Pigeons used to balance on the cables, their pink claws gripping the lines as they bobbed and cooed. Despite Komal telling him not to, he sometimes threw his shoe at them just to watch them burst into motion. And all these hundreds of cables looped down to the ground in a horrendous tangle at the telephone junction box.

He knew this junction box. Ma and Pa had warned him not to play with its cables.

Trying to stay calm, he walked past the junction box. He came to a fork in the alley and went left. The alley expanded into a small and empty parking lot where he and the children in the colony played seven stones. The surrounding walls were pockmarked with stains from the rubber ball they threw at each other. And there. There it was. Just beyond the parking lot, down a lane, and opposite a dead neem tree whose roots had split open the stone ground. There was the house he called home.

His legs trembled. He placed a hand on the front door and felt as though the bones in his body might turn to ash.

'Ma.'

A window next to the door blazed yellow. A shadow slid across its surface. The lock to the front door twisted open with a clack that he felt in his fingertips, and the door swung inwards.

Ma stood on the threshold. She was wearing her favourite shawl, the one Grandma had made for her, and it was like he'd travelled back in time to the evening when they'd made the gramophone.

From behind her came a roar. 'Is it him? Did he come?'

It was a voice he recognized. One that made him drop the stick and hold his hands to his chest.

'Did he come?' the voice boomed again, and there he was, filling up the doorway, squeezing past Ma and swooping down on Varun with ferocious joy. 'He did it! He's here!' Pa squeezed him tight, the solidity of him knocking the breath out of Varun.

Ma gasped. She wrapped her arms around the two of them, pressed her cool cheeks against his own, and laughed. Pa continued to bellow at the empty buildings. 'My boy's here! My boy! My boy!' And Varun could no longer hold it back. He wept into Ma's shoulder. He clung to his parents and they to him.

23

Usha listened to the sounds of the empty house. Despite it being the middle of the afternoon, a designated period of silence for residents of the road, construction continued in the adjacent plot. She wouldn't mind the noise so much if the builders simply obeyed the laws drafted by the residents' association. But no, they were beholden to their own bloody rules. Her husband would've hated the situation. When they first moved into the bungalow, there were only a few neighbouring houses, and the road had been a peaceful one-way where children played cricket in the evenings. If the children tried to do that now, they'd be run over in an instant.

She flinched. She was so stupid to think like that. So stupid. She could never think like that again. She hoped Varun wasn't crossing the road without telling them.

Poppy twitched awake beside her.

'How're you feeling?' she asked, stroking the dog's back. 'Any better?'

Poppy yawned, her tongue curling in her mouth. She lifted her snout to sniff the air.

'Come on,' Usha said. She led Poppy to the front door. Outside, the dog stood wary. Tensed to run, her eyes were wide and she kept cocking her head.

'What's the matter with you? Go on. Otherwise, I'll take you to the vet.'

She toed Poppy, who resisted at first, digging her heels in. But after nibbling a few blades of grass, she wandered towards the roots of the guava tree to take care of her business. Her fur rippled.

Usha, barefooted, relished the strong breeze whipping through her nightie. She smelled unpleasant, vinegary. Her underarms were clammy and her nightie clung to her back. She rummaged through her pockets and fished out a fistful of medicine tablets, dog biscuits, and throat lozenges. As Poppy toppled a nearby anthill, sending shiny black ants scattering in a million directions, she tossed a few biscuits to the ground and whistled.

The driveway was empty. She crunched on a lozenge till her jaw ached, and cursed herself. Jyoti must've just reached the BESCOM office. Hopefully, it wasn't very crowded and she could settle the bill quickly. Poor Jyoti. She truly was doing everything now. And who knew when Seema would return? Her husband was a good gardener, but he was also an alcoholic degenerate.

From the apartment complex came the shrieks of children playing. They too were not following the laws laid down by the residents' association. The parents were to blame. They should know better. The truth was the whole road was going to the dogs. She heard the tinkle of a bicycle bell and wondered if Varun wanted to join them. It was obvious that he was lonely. Once or twice she'd come across him hastily hanging up the landline, looking like a thief caught red-handed. The call log indicated a number in Delhi. Perhaps that Komal girl. The poor boy, he needed to be around other children, running and playing till he was exhausted and forgot what had happened. Yet she could understand Jyoti's reluctance to let him out of the house. She'd acted much the same way. The day she learnt that Jyoti was losing her sight, she refused to listen to the doctor and went to her local library instead. She thumbed through any and all books she could find on the blind. The photographs of clouded eyes stayed with her. The fact that India was home to the largest population of blind people in the world stayed with her. When she left the library, she kept her head down and avoided looking at people. And it took her so long to trust the world with Jyoti. The holes in the pavement, the overflowing sewers, the dangling electrical cables, the endless and roaring traffic, gossiping fishwives, and men who leered and men who teased and men who groped and men in general and all those other people who couldn't see beyond Jyoti's blindness.

Anu had accused her of strangling Jyoti's life.

She ran a hand through her thinning hair.

Poppy headed around the side of the house and she followed after the dog to the back garden where Jyoti's pottery wheel lay unused. All the clay had turned an ugly grey. She started. Poppy had let out a loud bark. The dog was standing with her tail stiff and her hackles raised.

'Yes? Tell me, what do you see? A bird? Or a squirrel?' Maybe it was the boy. Speaking of which, she hadn't seen him in a while. 'Varun?' She cleared her throat. 'Varun?' She glanced down the driveway and then opened the back door to check the house. There was no sign of him. Jyoti did have a point, where on earth was he disappearing off to?

24

While her ma was distracted, Poppy crept inside the grove. Weeds brushed her belly as she padded towards the tunnel. No one had told her. No one had mentioned the contaminating effects of a tunnel. Last night she'd suffered from dreams so frightfully real that she hadn't known if she was awake or asleep.

Her siblings.
The plastic bag.
The man knotting the handles.
The plummet.
The gutter.
The gutter water.
Her siblings clambering over her.
Darkness rising as they sank and all light was snuffed out.

Poppy scuffed the earth with her hind legs. Her ma had pulled her out of the dream. But what about the boy? Who would rescue him? He was visiting the tunnel too often now. The more he visited that place, the more he endangered them all. And what lay hiding in wait?

His scent was fresh. Perhaps he had only just entered. Perhaps she could stop him before he got lost, before something on the other side grabbed him by the legs and twisted him upside down.

She stopped. She could hear the hiss and crackle, the sounds so in contrast with the beauty of the world. Trees shivered in anticipation of rain, dragonflies hovered in the air, purple clouds were luminescent with lightning, and kites flew in ever-widening circles, trilling in delight at the untrammelled forces of a descending storm.

GO.

Poppy yelped.

GO AWAY.

Poppy yelped again and tucked her tail between her legs.

GO AWAY. AND DON'T COME BACK. If you do, I will stone you and beat you and grind you into mincemeat. Do you understand? I will choke you till the light in your eyes is MINE. Come back here and you will die. YOU WILL DIE.

Poppy fled.

The voice, like rocks scraping against each other, did not follow. She hurtled through the underbrush in such a panic that she fell twice, the world twisting above her in a jumble of limbs, branches, and sky. Only when the house was in sight, when the smell of her markings by the clothesline and guava tree joined ranks behind her, did she skid to a halt. She barked at the treeline. But what was the use? Her markings, her teeth, all the canine laws would not save her from that. She trembled. She'd urinated in fear and her hind legs were damp and streaked with mud.

Panting, she bent her head to her water bowl. Hundreds of insects were trapped under the surface of the water, unable to beat their wings and escape, pushed further down by the energy of their panic. Above her, insects battered themselves senseless against the wire-mesh windows.

Death had come to their doorstep.

But this was her home. Her home. All she had to do was scratch at the door and she'd be let inside. Safe and warm in her ma's arms. The scent of talcum powder protecting her. All she had to do was step away from these dead insects in her bowl of water. One step. It was a choice that was no choice at all. A boy in danger, or her ma, her sister, her own life.

25

Varun stepped inside. The chest of drawers in the hallway was cluttered with loose change and sheets of paper from Ma's work. The clock ticked on. His chest ached at the sound. Peering inside the office, he found the gramophone on the floor, its thin motor wires reaching for the battery. The record lay motionless, reflecting light. Hardest of all was passing the doorway to his parents' bedroom. Their bed was unmade. He'd lain in the dip of their mattress and waited for them to return, blanket over his head with the light from the hallway taking on a fiery shade of orange. Their bed was exactly as he left it when the police rang the doorbell.

'Everything okay?' Ma asked. She and Pa were watching him.

He tried to smile.

In the living room, the television screen reflected their silhouettes as they took their usual places. Ma sat on the sofa by the windows. Pa sank into his armchair. And Varun sat cross-legged on the carpet, where it had been worn thin from him playing with his toys while watching cartoons.

'What's the matter?' Ma asked.

'Nothing.'

'You can tell us. We won't bite your head off.'

'Nothing.'

Pa smiled. 'It doesn't take a genius to tell you're upset about something.'

Varun couldn't understand why he was feeling this way. It was what he wanted, wasn't it? He'd found Ma and Pa. They were all together again. Yet he continued to trace the geometric pattern on the carpet and yank out loose threads with a clenched fist.

'We know when something is bugging you,' Ma said.

'Nothing is bugging me.'

'Just tell us, no?'

'I... I'm confused.'

'About what?'

'Where are we?'

'What kind of question is that?' Pa said brightly. 'We're at home.'

But he wasn't so sure anymore. It was what he wanted to believe, he knew that now, but he could tell by Ma's expression that it wasn't true. They weren't in Bangalore. And they weren't in Delhi.

'If this is home, then where is everybody? What happened to the buildings?'

'Where do you think we are?' Pa asked, as though this was a homework problem they were sitting down to solve.

'I don't know.'

'Isn't this our living room?'

'I... yes?'

'Isn't this our house?'

'But what about Munirka? What happened to it?'

Pa glanced at Ma.

'I don't understand,' Varun said. 'How did you get here?'

Pa stood up and paced the living room in circles. 'Why are

you… there's no need for questions like that. We're here. And you're here. Right? We should be celebrating!'

It was odd hearing Pa speak in this cheery voice. The questions he'd asked were the questions Pa would expect of him during their field trips to heritage sites.

'Forget about this q-and-a session,' Pa said. 'Come on, what would you like to do? Tell us. Anything you-'

'Alok,' said Ma, cutting him off.

Pa stopped.

Ma slid down from the sofa and held Varun's hands in her own. 'It's difficult to explain,' she said.

And suddenly Varun's throat was painfully tight. When he spoke, it was in a cracked voice that sounded like somebody else. 'Ma, if you were here, why didn't you look for me? All this time, why didn't you come find me?'

'Oh, beta.'

'We did,' Pa protested.

'Alok.'

'I promise, we did! But-'

'Alok. Wait.'

With great effort, Pa kept quiet. He crossed his arms.

Ma's eyes glimmered as she spoke. 'That night… something happened that night, because one minute we were driving back to you, and the next we were in this place. It was very confusing for us. Munirka looked like it had been destroyed by an earthquake. We couldn't understand what had happened, couldn't process it, but the first thing we thought of was you. We ran back home and… you were gone.' She closed her eyes and shuddered. 'Can you imagine it, beta? To come back home and find it empty? No. No! It was the worst moment of my life.'

'But I was at home,' Varun whispered.

'We looked for you,' she continued. 'Maybe you'd left the house to find us? Or maybe you were in Komal's house. But no. It was like you'd vanished.'

'You were gone,' Pa said, his face sagging.

'We searched for you.'

'We banged on doors. We broke windows.'

'We screamed your name. We screamed till our throats were raw, and still we called out to you.'

'All we wanted was to find you. My god, we tore down everything.'

'Everything. Every building. Every house. Every room.' Ma's skin was so pale she glowed. Her face contorted, and Pa knelt to wrap an arm around her shoulders.

Varun could see the birthmark on his forearm. It was almost painful to hear his parents finish each other's thoughts like they always did. He wanted them to continue, even though what they said made no sense. He was the one who'd been left behind, not them.

'We were supposed to go to Mehrauli, remember?' Pa said.

They were. It had been one of the history lessons they'd planned for the month. There were many monuments there, including the Qutub Minar, but Pa wanted to walk through the old flower market that had survived a bomb blast. To show how hate could scar but love could endure.

'We can still go if you want,' Pa said. 'I promise not to make the trip too boring.'

'Don't make promises you can't keep,' Ma joked, though she didn't laugh.

'Okay, maybe no history lessons. Forget that. What about flying a kite? You've been wanting to do that for ages. We could do that. All three of us.'

Varun imagined standing in the middle of the ruined park with its uprooted trees, thread hissing between his fingers, a line unspooling into the sky. Ma explaining the physics of a kite and Pa tracing its history.

'Or we could go swimming?' Pa said.

'The pool's empty, Pa.'

'We'll fill it up. We can use the coin to play. See? We can do whatever you want. Your choice, beta.'

Varun didn't know what he wanted anymore.

'Here,' Ma said, lifting his chin. 'Come look at this.' She led him to his bedroom. There were his dioramas, his papier mâché science projects. Everything was as he remembered, save for one thing. Framed and hanging above the bed was his most recent painting.

'*Sitana ponticeriana*, found only on the Coromandel Coast,' he whispered. He'd spent weeks sketching its body and scales in pencil lines, before painting it with watercolours. Perched on craggy black rocks, and leaning back on delicate hindlegs so its nose pointed to the sky, his lizard had unfurled the loose skin under its neck into a fan of vibrant metallic hues.

Glued to the bottom of his painting was a silver star.

'I told you I'd frame it,' Ma said. 'It's your best work.'

'Even though it's a lizard,' Pa said.

Varun sat on his bed. He wished he could crawl under the blanket and fall asleep. Maybe when he woke up, everything would be back to normal and he could live here again. He thought of Jyoti Aunty. He'd made her a promise.

'Are you tired, beta?' Ma asked.

'Why don't you lie down?' Pa said. He picked up a copy of the book they were reading, the same copy which was also in Bangalore, and thumbed through its dusty pages. 'We can start a new chapter if you want.'

'Have you been reading it?' Varun asked.

'No. I waited. It was very hard, but I wanted to read it with you.'

'Oh.'

'Did you read it?'

'Just a few pages. I told Jyoti Aunty about it.'

'Jyoti Aunty?' Pa frowned. 'What did she think?'

'She said it sounded interesting.'

'And Grandma?'

'She doesn't talk to me that much.'

'So you're unhappy there? You don't like it there?'

'No, I…' He was surprised by the eagerness in Pa's voice. 'I don't know.'

'Hmm. Jyoti Aunty and Grandma. That old house.'

'And Poppy.'

'Oh yes. The dog.'

Varun fidgeted with the blanket. He felt as though he'd said something wrong.

'Jyoti Aunty said it sounded interesting,' Pa continued, smoothing the cover of the book, 'but she can't read it to you, can she?'

'No.'

'That's right. Because she's blind.'

Thunder rumbled past the house. Varun turned to Ma, but she'd obviously not heard because she was pulling two chairs to the side of the bed. Pa looked strange then, not smiling, his unblinking eyes staying on him. Varun wanted to ask him why he would say it like that, like it was a bad thing, but Ma gathered the shawl around her and Pa opened the book.

'Now then,' Pa said, still not smiling, 'where were we?'

26

Poppy lay panting under the earth, exhausted from digging. The topsoil was damp from the rains and she could feel it turn to sludge and fall in clods behind her. If she wasn't careful, she'd be buried alive.

I will choke you, the voice had said.

She sniffed the way forward. By now she should've passed under the crackling vertical line, but dimensions fluttered in front of her like curtains in a breeze and she'd lost all sense of direction. Everything felt so unnatural. Her body convulsed, as though she'd swallowed poison and her stomach was trying to expel it. Considering her state, there was only one option left. She burrowed upwards, kicking hard with her hindlegs.

Come back here and you will die.

A growing pressure made it difficult to breathe. The soil had congealed and was slimy against her fur, sliding between her teeth and down her throat. She retched. Her nose was blocked. She sneezed, wheezed, wriggled, and twisted, trying to dig her way out.

You will die.

But she was so close now. She writhed in panic and the soil gave way. Wind upon her face, lightning streaking across the sky, a sudden lightness, and at last she was dragging herself out of the earth's grip. She vomited hot green bile and collapsed on her side, breathing in shallow gasps.

She blinked away the grit in her eyes and took in her surroundings. She was in the middle of a park, one with trees that lay overturned, their roots reaching for the sky. The place reeked of death. There was nowhere to hide, the tunnel had tricked her into resurfacing in the open. And she could feel something was wrong inside of her. Strange aches and stabbing pains. There was a cost to crossing over.

What about the boy? Had the tunnel already trapped him?

She staggered to her feet. The hair on her back bristled. Something was watching her. A predator waiting in the shadows. Staying low, she crept out of the park. She found a road unlike any road she'd seen before, free of traffic and quiet, yet still brimming with menace. With her tail tucked between her legs, she limped down the pavement to the entrance of a courtyard.

The boy's scent was strong here. He'd crossed the road.

She retched. She retched again, unable to fully expel the poison that had taken root deep inside of her. Her legs trembled from the effort. She was tired. Too tired to save the boy. Too tired and too old. Her ears were shredded, pain riddled her insides, and her joints could no longer bear her weight. She crumbled to the ground and lay there, panting.

She didn't hear it or see it, but she sensed it. A charge to the air.

Something was nearing, crackling and sizzling.

Panic surged through her. She tried to rise to her feet but there was a burst of static and suddenly she was pinned to the ground. It was enormous, immovable, overwhelming her senses as it hissed and sputtered.

Found you, little digger.

Poppy yelped.

It crushed her with its full weight, and she scrabbled for purchase as her eyes rolled and dots burst across her vision. But it was impossible, hopeless. There was no escaping this. What little strength she had left was gone. The stones of the pavement were cold, their rough edges digging into her side as her life was being snuffed out. She thought of her ma by the gate, waiting for her to come home.

In this strange place, in this strange world, Poppy closed her eyes. There was a great rush of darkness.

27

Varun tried to listen to Pa read from the book, but he was too distracted by what Pa had said about Jyoti Aunty. Why would he say such a thing so cruelly? Ma didn't even tell him off. She was watching Varun. Her eyes hadn't left him since she sat down, and there was a strange expression on her face as though she was in pain. This was nothing like what he'd expected.

A flash of lightning illuminated the room. For an instant, both Ma and Pa seemed to disappear into thin air, and then thunder erupted around the house and they were silhouettes in the darkness. Varun started.

'What's wrong?' Pa asked.

'Nothing.'

'You must be tired. Why don't you try and sleep?'

'Over here?'

'Yes, over here. Where else? It's getting late.'

'But I...'

'What's the problem?'

'I just... don't I have to go back?'

'Go back? Why?'

'I told Jyoti Aunty-'

'Jyoti Aunty?' Pa's expression sharpened.

'I told her I'd be back soon.'

'You're here with us. You don't need to worry about Jyoti Aunty anymore, so what's the problem?'

'She'll be waiting for me. I made a promise.'

'But you're home.'

Varun turned to Ma.

'Pa's right,' she said. 'You're home.'

'You can't go now in any case,' Pa said. 'Not in this weather. I forbid it.'

'But Jyoti Aunty will worry.'

'And what about us?' Pa said, speaking in the same slow, soft tone of voice he used when he was angry. 'You don't mind if we worry?'

'No! No, I didn't-'

'But you don't want Jyoti Aunty to worry. Why would she worry, huh?'

'Pa, please, I-'

'She's blind, beta. She can't see. She can't read this book to you. Tell me, how can she take care of you if she can't even take care of herself? Half the time she walks into walls or trips over furniture. She'd be happy you're with us.'

Varun clenched his toes.

Pa imitated Jyoti Aunty clumsily walking into a wall and Ma laughed.

It was a short, sharp laugh, filled with cruelty he'd never heard before, and Varun knew in that moment that these people were not his parents. Their features were too pale, their voices coarse like rusted barbed wire.

'Please,' he said. 'I'll come back. I will.'

'This is your home. Why are you acting this way?'

'I told Jyoti Aun-'

'Jyoti Aunty, Jyoti Aunty. Is that all you can say?'

'No, I-'

'Enough.' Pa's beard bristled with anger. 'We're your parents. You will listen to us.'

Varun fidgeted with the bandage on his knee. 'You broke your promise.'

'What?'

But Varun was no longer speaking to Pa. He looked at Ma. 'You broke your promise. You told me you'd be home soon. But you never came back.'

Her eyes widened.

'You lied to me, Ma.'

She gaped at him, and he could see himself reflected in the depths of her eyes.

'After you left, I played with the gramophone. I'm sorry. I know you told me not to, but I was careful with the motor. I shouldn't have broken my promise, but you shouldn't have broken yours either. Maybe if I hadn't done it, if I'd been good... then maybe this wouldn't have happened.'

'No,' she whispered, shaking her head. 'Don't think like that. You're a good boy. The best. Even if you're a real troublemaker. Why do you want to go?'

Varun opened his mouth but couldn't speak. Ma looked so old then, small and afraid, clutching her shawl.

She nodded. 'Okay. If you think you should go, then go.'

'What?' Pa shouted. The light above him flickered.

'It's late, Alok. Let him go back.'

'Why?'

'Can't you see?'

'What the hell are you talking about?'

'He's right, Jo will be worried.'

'Jo will be worried? Jo? So what? What are you doing?'

She took Varun's hand and led him out. She opened the front door but hovered on the threshold. Wind gusted through the hallway.

'I'm sorry,' Varun said to her hand. He didn't understand any of this and hearing Pa shout at Ma made him want to hide in the smallest of spaces, to rewind time and go back to when they were all happy together.

Ma ran her hand through his hair. His body filled with a pleasant tingling sensation and he leaned against her.

'You've grown,' she said. 'You're taller. I can tell.'

'Can you come with me?' he asked. 'Can you both come with me?'

'No. You know we can't.'

'But you can stay,' Pa said.

'No, Alok.'

'What's the matter with you?' Pa shouted again.

Varun wanted to cover his ears. He wanted to run away but also stay with Ma, holding her hand and never letting go.

'You know the way back, beta?' Ma asked.

He nodded.

Pa's expression changed. His face softened. He knelt so that he was face to face with Varun and held him by the shoulders. 'I'm sorry if I frightened you, beta. I promise I didn't mean to. I was just so happy to see you. And I don't want to lose you again. Will you come back to us? Please, please come back. We're here, waiting for you.' He looked terrified, panicked. 'If it rains, maybe there'll be enough water for us to swim in the pool. We can search for the coin like we used to before. Wouldn't that be nice?'

'Alok,' Ma said.

'It was my wish. Did you know that? I went to the pool and flipped a coin and wished for you to be with us.'

'Alok, don't.'

But he's here!' Pa pleaded with her. 'We have to take care of him, Anu. He needs us.'

'Go, beta.'

'I don't know what to do anymore, Ma,' Varun said.

'Keep your promise.'

He picked up the stick and tentatively walked away, glancing back with every step. Ma stood by the doorway and Pa was slumped on the ground. When he reached the end of the lane they were gone and the door was shut. What was he doing? This was Ma and Pa. This was home. He stood there for a long time, his head buzzing as the clouds flashed and darkness gathered around him.

28

Jyoti waited by the corner of an intersection for the lights to change and the pedestrian signal to ring. Her head ached. It had taken a long time to settle the power bill because the government office had been swarming with customers complaining about similar payment-related issues. One horrid man even shoved past her to jump the queue. She'd struggled to keep her temper with the official who, midway through helping her, answered his phone to speak with his wife. After escaping that hellish place, she stopped at a pharmacy to purchase bandages, gauze, and antiseptic ointment, as well as a stainless-steel torch for Varun. It had a good grip. And a comforting weight. At least he could use it whenever there was a power cut or the generator died. Which was pretty much all the time nowadays.

The shrill pedestrian signal punctured her thoughts. There came the reluctant screech of brakes, followed by the usual cacophony of honks. Plenty of motorists accelerated instead of slowing down and zipped across the intersection. Nearby, girls attending an evening class at a college were discussing plans for the weekend. 'Sister?' one of them said and took her hand. Jyoti allowed herself to be led across the road and thanked the girl. The generosity of strangers often made her feel like a goat being led to a butcher's chopping block, but these college girls were kind. They didn't patronize her. And she liked that they called her sister. It reminded her of how she and Anu used to walk together with their arms interlinked.

Despite the countless pujas she'd performed for her parents, she'd never been a religious person. But she wished she could speak with Anu's spirit. Or just Anu herself. It would be so nice to hear her voice again, to talk over the phone about the boring everyday activities that filled their lives. There was no point to it, of course, but she called Anu.

We're sorry. This number is no longer operational.

Click.

She dialled again and got a different message.

The number you have dialled is incorrect. Please try again.

Click.

Jyoti stopped walking. Standing in the middle of the pavement, she scrolled through her messages, concentrating on the phone's automated voice as she searched and searched and searched till she found a voice message Anu had sent a few months back.

Oi, what are you doing? Too cool for me? Can't message me?

Jyoti replayed the message seven times, listening to her sister tease her till every breath was a gasp and she was relieved she was wearing her dark glasses.

When she reached home, the front gate croaked open as it always did, but Jyoti felt like she was crossing a barrier into a foreign world. Weeds had grown wild, brushing against her ankles, and the birds in the trees chittered non-stop. She found Mama sitting outside, sipping a cup of tea. She smelled nice, like she'd taken a shower and scrubbed off days of sweat and grease.

'Are you okay?' Mama asked.

'I'm fine. Just tired.'
Mama took her hand.
'Paid the electricity bill?'
'Yes.'
'Thank you.'
'Okay.'

She stood like that, holding hands with Mama, listening to the deepening rumbles of thunder. The trees swayed and swished with every gust of wind. A door in the house slammed with a bang.

'Lots of lightning,' Mama said.

'The air is so stuffy. I need to take a bath.'

'If the bill's been paid, then the power should be back. You can turn on the geyser.'

Despite the approaching rain, children in the neighbouring apartment complex continued to shriek and laugh, trying to squeeze in as much playtime as they could before their parents leaned over balcony railings to call them home.

'Where's Varun?'

'Playing.'

'I'd better get him. Sounds like it's going to rain like mad.'

She squeezed Mama's hand and walked around the guava tree to the back garden. 'Varun?'

There was no response.

'Varun? Where are you?'

She sat in one of the patio chairs and spun the pottery wheel. It groaned on its axle. She tapped her shoes with her cane. The grove was the one place everyone forbade her from visiting when she lost her vision. *Too dangerous*, Mama insisted. *You'll fall and hurt yourself*, Papa said, patting her arm. And after a point, even Anu didn't want her wandering through the grove. It became the place where she and her classmates smoked or drank beer. And did who knows what else? Once, when Jyoti tried to eavesdrop on them, she tripped over a root and sprained her ankle. Which, of course, infuriated everyone in the family.

'Varun!' Mama shouted.

'I'm sure he'll be back soon.'

She'd forgotten she was still carrying the paper bag from the pharmacy. Hopefully, she wouldn't need the antiseptic ointment this evening. Though there was the boundary wall with its shards of glass. When had he last had his tetanus shot? She needed to find the folder with his medical records. Another high-priority task for the checklist. She rubbed her forehead.

'Did Anu and I give you lots of trouble when we were children, Mama?'

'Of course. What do you think?'

'I guessed as much.'

'But that's normal, no?'

Mama shuffled to the house. Jyoti bent her head towards the grove, listening hard.

'Varun!' she tried again. 'Where are you? Come on! Time to come back!'

Even as the first drops began to fall, Jyoti remained outside, trying to discern through the pitter-patter the sound of footsteps returning home.

29

Varun peered through the flashing ribbons of rain at the junction box. Ma and Pa had warned him not to touch the box or the black cables that criss-crossed the sky above him and swung with a life of their own. Ma and Pa who'd behaved so strangely and said such cruel things. Ahead of him was an overflowing gutter. Behind him was home.

What was he doing?

Keeping a promise, said the coin.

Being good, said the stick.

They were right. Or were they?

Come on.

Hurry.

He sloshed down the alley, taking care not to trip as his shoes grew heavy with water. He was soon drenched. His hair was plastered against his forehead and his shirt clung to his back. Chills racked his body. He clambered over a pile of rubble and was suddenly drained of all energy. He swayed, caught hold of a street sign and held on to it for support.

You can do it.

You're almost there.

Varun stumbled into a gutter.

One step at a time.

Lean on me.

And he did. Leaning on the stick, he staggered to the end of the alley. The road that he'd crossed had transformed into a shallow stream. Overturned streetlights lay half-drowned in the muddy waters, their slender metal necks just above the surface. Listening to his companions' gentle words of encouragement, he crossed the road, tapping the ground in front of him to make sure he didn't fall into a pothole.

He wished for bed and sleep. Why hadn't he stayed at home? Pa had been midway through a chapter of the book. Ma could've tucked him in. He remembered Ma's vicious laugh and the way Pa had shouted at her. He'd left because something was wrong. They were them but not them.

We're here.

We made it.

They were in the courtyard. The pool rippled with grey water. Pa hadn't been wrong. The next time, they could go swimming.

Careful.

Keep an eye on the shadows.

Varun nearly laughed. After what he'd just experienced, what would it matter if the shadows moved? But before he could respond, he spotted something lying in a heap by the wall.

'No,' he breathed.

Her fur was drenched, slathered in streaks of mud.

He sat next to her, not wanting to touch her because doing so would make this real. But when he did run his fingers through her fur, he was shocked to find she was cold. 'Poppy,' he said, cradling her and trying not to cry. This was his fault. She must've come after him. She must've tried to help him. 'Please wake up.' Her body was so limp it felt boneless.

This is serious.
Help her.
'How?'
Take her to a doctor.
Take her back.

Varun swallowed his panic. He nodded and faced the wall. The hole wasn't there but he knew what he needed to do. He needed to take Poppy back to the bungalow. He needed to find Jyoti Aunty and Grandma. It was what he wanted. More than anything else in the world. A crack appeared. Bricks turned to powder. The hole formed in front of him.

It happened then. His shoulders tensed as the air behind him crackled with energy. Before he could even turn around, he felt a horrendous pinch in his calf, so hard that it made him gasp and nearly drop Poppy. It was only for a second, like the jab of a needle, but pain sizzled its way through his body.

And then it was over. He rubbed his calf, bright red in one spot but otherwise unharmed. What was that?

There's no time.
Remember Poppy!

They were right. The hole was wide enough now. He gingerly climbed through it and then, with what little energy he had left, he ran, weaving past trees and clutching Poppy tight and whispering into the soft folds of her ears, 'Hold on, Poppy, hold on.' When he reached the bungalow and stepped under the light of the front porch, he was too preoccupied to notice that he cast an extra shadow.

30

The doorbell rang three, four, five times.

'Why so many times?' Usha complained to her cup of tea. She knew Varun must be soaked from the rain, but that didn't mean he had to bring down the house with that infernal racket.

'Coming, coming,' Jyoti said, shuffling past her room to open the front door.

Usha set aside her newspaper. The front door opened, and the hiss of rain intensified and then diminished with a click. She couldn't understand what Varun was saying, but he was speaking very fast, his voice rising as Jyoti told him to calm down. What on earth had happened? With a groan, she climbed out of bed and went to investigate.

She gasped.

Varun was standing by the door, drenched, dripping water everywhere. And in his arms was Poppy, her body limp and her tongue lolling out of her open jaws.

'What is this?' She pushed aside Jyoti and grabbed Poppy. Her dog was stone-cold. 'What happened? What did you do?'

'Mama-'

'I didn't do anything, Grandma.'

'Look at her! Tell me what you did!'

'I found her like this. I promise.'

'Where?'

'Back there. By the... by the wall. She was lying on the ground. Not moving.'

'The wall? What utter nonsense! Tell me the truth!'

'Mama! No need to speak like–'

'Jyoti, for once in your life, hold your tongue!' She yanked a towel from the linen cupboard and wrapped Poppy in it, trying to warm her little body. This was her Poppy. She'd rescued her. What had happened?

'Mama, will you–'

'I want you to call me a cab. Now. I need to take her to the vet. I told you we needed to take her to the vet. I told you. But you never listen. You're so stubborn. You think you're always right.'

'Just wait a second, Mama. Is she hurt? Check.'

'Check, check, check, you can't see and I'm telling you she's hurt. Just call me a cab.' She laid Poppy down on the table and inspected the fur behind her neck, under her snout. There were no cuts or wounds. No blood. There didn't appear to be any visible injuries. Then what? She was old, was it possible she'd had a heart attack? Usha tried to find a pulse but she didn't know where to check and her hands shook. She took a deep breath, calmed herself, and watched Poppy's chest.

It rose. It fell.

'Jyoti!'

'The app says the cab is on its way.' She was holding the phone close to her ear and listening to that damned automated voice.

'Give me that,' she said, snatching the phone from Jyoti's hands. The cab was at the top of the road. It would reach in less than a minute. She dropped the phone on the table and raced to get an umbrella. She crammed a bottle of water and some tissues inside her handbag, checked she had her purse and phone, then lifted Poppy into her arms and rushed out into the rain.

Jyoti called after her, but Usha didn't stop. She hurried down the driveway, slipping but regaining her balance. The rain intensified, turning the world white around her, and she cursed the weather, the gods, Bangalore traffic, and stupidly reckless boys. Not bothering to close the gate behind her, the same gate where she used to feed Poppy when she was a stray, she climbed into the cab. The driver frowned at the sight of Poppy, and Usha snapped, 'Let's go, let's go, quickly!'

31

Jyoti took out a towel from the storage cupboard and wrapped it around Varun's shoulders. She rubbed his arms up and down, trying to warm him up. He was trembling. 'Go to your room,' she said. 'Change your clothes. Dry your hair. Then come back here, please. I want to talk to you.'

'Okay.'

She tapped the floor with her cane. She untied her hair, which was thick and frizzy, and retied it into a painfully tight knot. What this situation required was calm. Mama had already screamed and shouted and charged out of the house with such drama. That would be enough to upset any child. What she needed to do was keep her temper. Even though Varun had been gone for more than four hours. Even though he'd returned in the middle of a downpour. God, why were children so infuriating?

She heard him move quietly around her.

'Okay,' she said, drawing a deep breath. 'First things first. You're not hurt, are you?'

'No.'

'I don't want you to lie to me. You can tell me the truth. I won't punish you for that.'

'I'm not hurt, Jyoti Aunty,' he whispered.

'Good. I'll change your bandages in a bit, they must be

soaked. Now explain yourself. What happened to Poppy? Do you know? And why were you gone for so long?'

'I was just playing.'

'In the rain?'

He didn't answer.

'Where were you?'

'By the wall.'

'What were you doing by the wall?'

No answer.

'Have you been climbing over the wall?'

No answer.

'Have you?'

'No.'

'Varun, there are sharp pieces of glass on that wall. You can hurt yourself. And there's construction going on in the neighbouring plot. Builders don't like it when people trespass.'

'I didn't climb the wall. I didn't know I wasn't allowed to play.'

'I never said that. Please don't put words in my mouth. What game were you playing that you couldn't come back home after it started raining?'

'I'm sorry.'

'No, Varun, that's just not good enough. I asked you a question and I want you to answer it. Tell me, please.' He didn't respond, and Jyoti was about to repeat her question when he spoke.

'There's a bougainvillea there.'

'A bougainvillea?'

'Ma always liked them.'

A flash of her sister as a child, stretching, standing on her toes and reaching for the thin and tender branches above her. 'That's right. She liked their pink flowers.'

He said something she didn't quite catch.

'What?'

'Not flowers. Bracts. Their bracts are pink.'

Rain beat against the windows. It was pouring harder than ever and thunder crackled and boomed in the distance. Her phone rang, but she muted the call. 'What about Poppy?'

'I promise, I found her like that.'

'By the wall.'

'Yes.'

'She doesn't go that far away from the house. Especially when it rains.'

He kept quiet.

'Were you playing with her?'

'No.'

'She's old. You know that, no? Were you making her play fetch or run around a lot? Or did you... did you hurt her?' Hadn't she had a conversation with Anu about this? Anu had once found Varun under a parked car, growling and swiping at a stray cat he'd cornered, terrifying it to provoke a reaction. 'While playing? Sometimes by accident we can be a bit rough with animals. You can tell me. I won't be angry. I just need to know because it could help her.'

'I would never hurt Poppy,' he said in a choked voice.

'Okay.'

He hiccoughed.

She listened to that sad little sound leap out of his body again. He was just a little boy. She crossed the room and pulled him into a hug. His hair was still damp.

'I told you not to get into trouble,' she said.

'But I kept my promise.'

She rubbed his back. 'Have a glass of water. And I know

your grandmother forgot to say it because she was so worried, but thank you for bringing Poppy back home. God only knows what would've happened if you hadn't found her.'

Varun said nothing to that. He left.

His story didn't add up. Anu had mentioned that he was prone to telling obvious lies. His denials about stealing were the worst. Anu had even gotten into the habit of counting how much money was in her purse, and she hated herself for it. Jyoti too had found herself doing the same. Was he sneaking off the property to buy things from a nearby store?

Her phone rang again. Who was it? Who kept calling in the middle of a downpour? The automated voice on her phone declared the name of the caller.

She sighed and tried to collect herself. 'Hi, Praveen.'

'I've been thinking,' he said in his rough voice, 'about our previous conversation.'

'Yes?'

'And I think what I would like most right now would be to fly somewhere peaceful. Any recommendations?'

'I...'

'It could be anywhere in the world.'

It was somehow the most ridiculous question she could imagine in that moment.

'Oh, this is not a good time,' he said.

'No.'

'Anything I can do to help?'

'No. It's okay.'

'Do you want to talk about it?'

'No. Later, maybe. I'm still trying to process what's going on.'

'Something to do with Varun?'

'Yeah.'

She heard him take a drag from his cigarette and exhale.

'Boys are difficult to take care of. We never listen. We always think we're right.'

'Tell me about it.'

'You know, it sounds like I'm not the only one who needs to fly somewhere peaceful. What do you think of the Andamans?'

'I've never been.'

'It's supposed to be good fun.'

She knew she needed to get off the line and untangle the evening's events, check on Mama and Poppy, on Varun, but there was an irresistible allure to the idea of escaping to a sun-drenched island. 'Anu flew to Port Blair a few years ago. From there she took a ferry to Havelock. She told me it was her favourite place in India. The roads were empty and Alok taught her how to ride a rented scooter. All they did was lie on the beach, swim, read crappy books, and stuff themselves with seafood and beer.'

'Sounds perfect.'

'I thought so too.'

'Well, I better book my tickets. Want to come along?'

'Me?'

'Definitely. A holiday would do you good. We'll have fun. Remember fun?'

'I think you're forgetting this strange thing called reality.'

'Nonsense.'

It was tempting to say yes, even if she knew they were playing pretend. To have her skin warmed by the sun, to push her toes under sand, or walk along the shoreline as the tide washed over her feet. 'I wish,' she said.

'Me too.'

'I have to go.'

'Sure. I understand.'

'Everything okay with you?'

He exhaled hard into the phone, filling the line with a crackle of static. 'Perfect.'

'I'm sorry.'

'Not your fault. It's the same old stuff.' He was silent for a few seconds, then asked, 'What was your father like?'

Her first thought was about their car. Papa had driven her to the AFB every day for two years despite it being in the opposite direction to his office. As he drove with the windows down and the traffic blaring, he'd follow common bus routes and test her memory, asking her where they were and what landmarks they were passing till her sense of direction was as keen as a compass. In the evenings they'd go for a walk, on the pretext of picking up dessert, and together would map the terrain of their neighbourhood. Sometimes he'd say, 'Stop,' and then tie her shoelaces. Unlike Praveen's father, Papa was patient and kind. He'd only wanted what was best for her.

Varun was in the kitchen. There was the glug of air travelling up the length of a bottle as water sloshed inside a glass. The sounds pulled her back to the present.

'I have to go,' she said.

'Okay. Sure.'

'Talk to you later. I'm sorry things are difficult at home.'

'Bye.'

The line died and Jyoti listened to Varun swallow water and gasp for air.

32

Usha sat humming in the vet's clinic. She stroked Poppy's back. The poor thing's tail was curled between her legs. She was trying to blink away the effects of the sedative.

'I'm sorry, my baby,' Usha said. She let out an irritable huff and glared at the vet.

'Just two more minutes, ma'am.'

Usha didn't dignify him with a response. Shaking her head, she dabbed a tissue against her tongue and teased grit out of the corner of Poppy's eye. Her coat was filthy and had ruined the towel. For the umpteenth time, she wondered what had happened to her. When Poppy was younger she roamed the property, but now her territory had shrunk to the guava tree and back garden. No, there was something strange going on. Even her behaviour when they arrived at the clinic had been alarming. Poppy never liked visits to the vet, but she'd awoken and howled at the ceiling, baring her teeth at anyone who approached her. When Usha placed her on the metal examining table, she'd urinated and, snapping her jaws, backed away from the vet till she nearly fell off.

'Don't worry, this happens, it's normal,' the vet had said.

But it wasn't normal for Poppy.

Why had she come here? All these doctors were fools. From

the fool who misdiagnosed Jyoti's degenerative eye disease to the fool who never spotted her husband's impending heart attack. They were useless. She muttered a silent prayer for her dog, but before she could finish, Poppy went limp in her arms.

Usha stroked her. She was reminded of the night she'd flown to Delhi to meet with the police and collect Varun. Neither of them wanted to sleep but both were exhausted. They'd sat on the living room couch. Eventually, Varun had lain his head against her thigh and she'd draped her arm over his chest. He'd been so tense that she'd wondered if he would ever relax and fall asleep. The next morning she'd woken up to an empty room and a sore back.

'Come, ma'am,' the vet said.

For some reason, he was wearing a surgical mask. Behind him was the examining table, a glass bottle filled with yellow liquid, and an array of sharp, shiny tools.

33

Anu stood in Varun's bedroom. His blanket lay rumpled across the bed and she wanted to press her palms into the mattress to see if it was still warm from his body. But she didn't. Why risk disappointment? Especially in this place.

The clock in the hallway ticked on.

Alok was keeping to himself. The foundation of their relationship was built on open communication, so silence was his way of punishing her. If she were to sit next to him now, he'd shake his head, rise, and depart. Leaving her alone with her guilt.

Or maybe Alok wouldn't even notice her and would continue to sit in his armchair, his expression wistful, lost in his dreams.

When they first arrived in this place, this destroyed Munirka, they'd been filled with such an all-consuming urgency to find Varun. But after they searched the colony and their energy fizzled out, they returned to this house. Because where else could they go? They drifted through these empty rooms like ghosts. They slumped into chairs and imagined the sound of Varun's footsteps bouncing off the walls. They dreamt. It was the only way of nurturing hope.

And then one day they both woke up from the same

dream. Of Varun resting his forehead against a crumbling wall and whispering, *I want to go home.* Since then, they'd sensed his arrival, tasted it.

The framed painting hanging over Varun's bed was askew, and as she adjusted it, she caught sight of her reflection in the glass. She closed her eyes and tried not to think about how much she'd aged in this place. There were streaks of grey in her hair and fine lines around her mouth. Her skin was pale and translucent.

No wonder Varun had looked so frightened. She and Alok were hardly recognizable. Varun had asked to leave. And she'd opened the door for him.

But just before he left, there'd been a moment. Varun had been fidgeting with his bandage and he'd whispered, *You broke your promise.* Her vision cracked when he uttered those words. She was there, sitting in front of her boy, and she was in Bangalore, in the old bungalow, holding Jo's hand while Mama blinked at the ceiling, and Papa knelt in front of them to repeat what the eye doctor had said. How Jo's life was going to change, their lives were going to change, but that they'd get through everything together as a family. *Promise.*

She didn't know if Varun would come back, but she knew that the moment had changed her, changed everything. It was like their roles had been reversed, and Varun had opened a door for her to walk through. It was her choice now, her decision. To stay here in this place of shadows and ruins, or to step through that door, to cross over.

34

Varun pretended to be asleep when Jyoti Aunty came to check on him. For the first time in his life, he was glad she couldn't see. In the dim light that came through the windows, he watched his calf muscles squirm under the skin. They'd been doing this since he returned from the place beyond the wall. He massaged his calf, but the muscles continued to painfully move with a life of their own. It was like trying to hold a bag of writhing snakes.

There were consequences to crossing over.

First Poppy.

Now him.

Who was next?

His parents should've told him everything. His parents who were not his parents. Those people who were shadows of Ma and Pa.

He drifted into an uneasy sleep. Twice he woke up in the night. First, when the front door opened and the hushed voices of Jyoti Aunty and Grandma passed his room. Second, when he thought he'd wet the bed. He clutched at his pyjamas to stop the sickly warmth from spreading across his thighs, but his pyjamas were dry and so too were the sheets. He went to the bathroom to avoid any accidents. But when he climbed back into bed, he still felt the need to urinate.

He tossed and turned, trying to get comfortable, then froze. In the darkest corner of the room, where the shadows were deep, stood the silhouette of a boy. He was watching him. Varun clenched his toes. There was a prickly charge in the air and his entire body was tensed to run. He stared into the corner, into the depths of the shadows, and the silhouette of the boy moved towards him.

Varun leapt out of bed and thudded down the hallway to Jyoti Aunty's room.

She was asleep. He shook her shoulder.

'Hmm? What is it?' she mumbled. 'Who– Varun? What's wrong?' She reached for her phone and the automated voice announced the time. 4.20 a.m. 'What happened?'

'Can I sleep here tonight?'

'Did you have a nightmare?'

'There's someone in my room.'

'What? Who?'

'I don't know.'

She frowned and blinked away her sleep. 'Okay.'

He waited for her to lift the blanket so he could crawl under it, but she got up instead, put on her slippers, and took his hand.

'Come on,' she said. 'Let's go check your room.'

'What if he's still there?'

'Here,' she said, handing him her cane. 'You hold that, and I'll turn on all the lights. If there's someone around, you can give them a whack.' She flicked on the hallway light. 'Anyone there?'

'No.' He kept his eyes on his bedroom doorway.

'Okay. Ready?'

He gripped her cane, ready to swing hard.

The room was empty.

'Anyone there?' she asked again.

'No.'

'Shall I check the bathroom?' She did it anyway, then checked behind the curtains and inside the wardrobe. She took the cane from him and waved it under the bed. 'I think you're safe.'

He didn't feel that way. 'Sorry for disturbing you, Jyoti Aunty.'

She yawned. 'Don't be silly. Tell you what, we know this room is safe, but now I'm a bit worried, so why don't you stay with me tonight?'

'Okay.'

They returned to her bedroom and she helped him get into bed. It was nice and warm. She lay next to him. He knew she was awake because she kept yawning and turning her ear in his direction. He was exhausted, but sleep wouldn't come. Despite the drawn curtains, Jyoti Aunty's room was lit up by the glare of fluorescent lights from the nearby apartment complex. He could see her table, her laptop, the shelves above displaying her collection of pottery.

'What are you thinking about?' she asked, her voice muffled by the blanket.

'Did you make all this pottery by yourself?'

'No. Not all. Some are gifts from my students.'

'Which ones?'

'There's this girl called Rukmini who made a clay mountain for me. On the lower shelf.'

'I see it.'

'It's nice, no? There are lovely patterns on one slope, and on the other side is a farmer's house and field.'

Varun pictured Rukmini as Komal.

'The top shelf has pottery I made. Very boring stuff. Plates and cups and bowls.'

'Is it difficult to make them?'

'Not really. I mean, as with anything, it takes practice. Aunty Zarina has a friend who's been helping me learn.'

'Isn't it messy?'

'I like the messiness.'

'You like the messiness, Jyoti Aunty?'

'Yes, mister sarcasm, I like the messiness. Not inside the house. But definitely in pottery workshops and in the studio. You'd love my apron. It's filthy!'

'Is it a lot of fun?'

'Oh, it's one of my favourite things to do.'

'How come?'

She thought about this for a while. 'I like to use my hands,' she said, speaking slowly, as though she too was trying to figure out the answer. 'I like to feel the shape of something take form. Even if it's an unexpected form. Bowls may be misshapen and plates may be wonky, but that doesn't matter. They're mine. Things went from my imagination to reality. That's like magic, no? All you need is a lump of clay and water, and you can make something out of nothing.'

Varun remembered bending his ear to the gramophone, listening for the faint voices of ghosts. He thought about what Jyoti Aunty had said. 'So, plates and bowls are magic?'

She chuckled. 'Very funny.'

'I like the bottle.'

'Which one?'

'The blueish-greenish one that looks like a jug.'

'That's a jug, silly.'

'Oh. Maybe you should put it in the living room and keep flowers in it.'

'We can do that if you like. Were you thinking bougainvillea?'

'Maybe. Yeah. Okay.'

'Okay.'

'Is Poppy better now?'

'I think so. I hope so. The vet said nothing was wrong with her, but she's getting old. It's not a good sign, finding her unconscious.'

'I don't want her to die.'

'No. I don't want her to die either. The house wouldn't be the same without her.'

'Houses change after people die.'

It was what Grandma had told him after an evening in Munirka, watching Pa's distant relatives argue over the house, the furniture, Ma's jewellery. How quickly the rooms had been stripped of their possessions. He'd recognized none of his relatives, and none of them had been interested in him.

'Yes,' Jyoti Aunty said. 'You're right. Houses change after people die. People do too. Things are so different for the three of us. But we have each other.'

He didn't say anything.

'And they're still with us, you know?'

He held his breath.

'They stay with us. Here,' she said, touching the side of his head, 'and here', she said, touching his chest, just above his heart. 'The people we love are never gone. We keep them alive.'

Everything in his body tightened. He couldn't move, couldn't speak. In the silence that followed, Jyoti Aunty held his hand.

'Since neither one of us is sleepy,' she said, 'shall we listen to something?'

'Listen to what?' he said, his voice hoarse.

She reached for her phone and earphones. 'Here,' she said, giving him the right earphone. She plugged the left earphone into her own ear. She pressed play and a man with a British accent spoke.

Chapter 31. The Story of El-ahrairah and the Black Rabbit of Inlé.
The power of the night, the press of the storm,
  The post of the foe;
Where he stands, the Arch Fear in a visible form,
  Yet the strong man must go.

'Oh!' he gasped, bumping his head against hers.
She grinned.
It was the same chapter he was on. She'd found his book. She'd caught up with him. The first few words were difficult to hear because his not-Pa had read them out last evening, but then they continued past that section and he felt the tightness in his chest loosen up. He closed his eyes and squeezed her hand. She squeezed back, and within minutes he was fast asleep.

35

Jyoti scrolled through her phone and listened to random voice messages from Anu.

What was the name of that dhobi who burnt your blouse?

Got a call from Mama. Why don't you come stay with us for two weeks?

Alok and I are thinking of going to Cochin for our anniversary. What do you think? Will it be too rainy this time of the year?

I miss Papa.

Sorry, can't talk right now, I'm late for work and Varun made such a scene this morning! I practically had to throw him into the school bus in front of all the other parents. Great gossip for the aunty brigade.

Two days! In two days I see your face!

Jyoti kissed her phone.

Around her, the house was in chaos. Seema hadn't turned up. The laundry hamper was full of stinking muddy clothes, there were dishes to be washed, food to be cooked, and floors to be swept. She considered going back to bed.

Varun was in his room. He'd stayed in there all morning, clicking Lego pieces together or spinning a coin across the floor. She wasn't sure where this coin had come from, but she didn't have the heart to interrogate him. Everyone was feeling a bit bruised.

She walked past Mama's bedroom.

'I told you we needed to take Poppy to the vet.'

'Yes, Mama, I know. But you told me the vet said nothing was wrong with her.'

'That fool. What does he know? You didn't see her.'

'Very nice.'

'Oh, please. He didn't even give her any medicine. Prescribed rest and relaxation. She's a dog! She's not going on vacation to Coorg, the fool.'

'Okay, Mama.'

'Okay, Mama, okay, Mama. I told you we should've taken her to the vet.'

'And now you're cursing the vet.'

'You don't understand. You can't see her.'

'Please stop saying that.'

'She's not moving now.'

'Is she resting?'

Mama clicked her tongue.

'What do you want me to do? Tell me,' Jyoti asked.

'Nothing. Go away.'

'Fine.'

Mama kept to her room, Varun to his, and Jyoti too stayed in her room. She closed the door and searched through the embossed labels she'd glued to her CD cases. She found the right CD, slid it inside the music system, plugged her earphones in, and cranked up the volume. A flash of her sister pulling her through a crowd, the heaving sensation of people moving and murmuring around her, the smell of beer, the stink of smoke, and then the music, the music and her and Anu jumping and dancing and singing along.

Someone tugged at her shirt.

'Ah! Varun?'
'Sorry, Jyoti Aunty.'
'What is it?'
'You were dancing.'
'Very observant.'
'Can I listen?'
'Sure.'

She yanked the earphones out of the system and music filled the room. The album was by an indie band whose hit song had recently been picked up for a television show. But at the time of the concert, they were only playing at small venues. Anu and Alok knew the drummer.

'What do you think?'
'It's okay.'
'You don't like them?'
'It's okay.' The bed creaked.
She sat next to him. 'What's up?'
'Nothing.'

'Oh, I forgot.' She rummaged through her bags and handed him the torch.

'For me?'
'Yeah. In case of a power cut.'
There was a click, a double-click, and a click again.
'Works?'
'It's really good. Thanks, Jyoti Aunty.'
'No problem.'
There was a double-click, a click, and a double-click again.
'Can we listen to the book?'

'Sure. You like the audio version, huh?' She paired her phone with the speakers. 'Ready?' Before she could press play, her phone rang. It was Zarina.

'How's it going?' Zarina asked.

'It's fine.'

'So, catastrophe after catastrophe, then?'

She snorted.

'I wanted to let you know,' Zarina continued, 'Hema is coming over with me today.'

'What?'

'She wants to talk to you. Is that okay?'

Jyoti thought about the grant application and the mountain of housework. They hadn't ticked off even half the things on her checklist. And her wrist was still swollen.

'It... I guess it should be fine.'

'Don't break your head trying to put together anything. We'll bring snacks.'

'Okay.'

'But I want a nice cup of ginger tea when I get there, please. Extra sugar.'

'No problem.'

'Cool. See you in the evening.'

Jyoti hung up and pressed play. The very British voice picked up from when Varun had fallen asleep, but she was too distracted by the pain in her wrist to follow along. Her mind was leaping from task to task, scenario to scenario. Did they have ginger? How messy was the living room? And why was Hema visiting the weekend before she was planning to return to work?

36

Varun helped Jyoti Aunty tidy the house. He swept the floors, separated colours from whites for the washing, and stacked old newspapers. He also offered to cut cucumbers and tomatoes, but Jyoti Aunty waved him away. She rewarded him with a bar of chocolate. It had almonds, but he didn't complain.

In the evening, two guests arrived. One was Aunty Zarina, shouting for a cup of tea as she pinched his cheeks. The other was a woman with a deep voice and short silver hair that glinted. Like Jyoti Aunty, she too waved a cane in front of her as she walked. There was something about the way she stood and spoke that made it clear she didn't tolerate any nonsense. Jyoti Aunty kept calling her ma'am.

She introduced herself as Hema. 'I heard you helped your aunt clean up the house. You must be quite a responsible young man.'

Jyoti Aunty patted his shoulders and he said, 'Thank you, ma'am.'

For some reason all three women chuckled.

'That's okay. And you may call me Hema if you want. I keep telling these two to do the same.'

He couldn't imagine calling her by her first name.

'Well, we're here to talk to your aunt. Would you like to join us?'

'You don't have to if you want to relax,' Jyoti Aunty said.

'Yes, please.'

'Go on then.'

He retreated to his bedroom and half-shut the door. He played with his new torch. It was made of metal, heavy and reassuring.

Click. A circle of light appeared on the ceiling. It slid down the wall to his study table, disappeared at the window, and reappeared on the carpet.

Double-click.

Click.

Double-click.

Click. Go through the wall.

Double-click. Stay here and put an end to the consequences.

Click. But his parents were waiting for him. Ma. Pa.

Double-click. Not-Ma. Not-Pa. They weren't them.

Click. They were real. Pa had carried him. Ma had run her hand through his hair.

Double-click. What about Poppy? What about Grandma and Jyoti Aunty?

Click.

Double-click. What if something bad happened to them?

Click. Then what? Never go back there again?

Double-click. Maybe.

Click. How could he abandon Ma and Pa? Even if they were not-Ma and not-Pa.

Double-click. And Jyoti Aunty?

Click. She'd understand.

Double-click. She'd wonder what happened to him. She'd think he ran away.

Click.
Double-click.
Click.
Double-click.

The power died. The generator whirred to life and then died. Gusts of wind rattled the windows. It looked like it was going to rain again. Inside, he could hear chairs moving. Jyoti Aunty came to check on him. She made space on the study table and placed a lit candle there for him.

Click. 'Thanks, Jyoti Aunty.'

'Oh yes, you have your torch now. Still, save the battery and use the candle, okay? You want to join us? We've got biscuits.'

Double-click. 'No thanks.'

She slid her way out of the room and soon the women continued their conversation. Varun watched the candle flame flicker. His calf muscles ached in the darkness and he could feel them twitch and squirm. Not wanting to be alone, he took the candle with him to Grandma's room.

'Jyoti?'

'It's me, Grandma.'

'Oh.'

The candle flame gave off a yellow glow that warmed the room. It softened the lines in Grandma's face, though her eyes reflected the light, reminding him of not-Ma beyond the wall. He dribbled wax on the side table and stood the candle on it.

'How's Poppy?' he asked.

'She's resting.'

He went around the side of the bed to check. She was on Grandma's lap, her head and body covered by the blanket, and her snout with its fading white hair poking out. He wanted to kiss her nose.

'Can I stay here till the power returns?'

Grandma inspected his face. 'Fine.'

He sat down cross-legged at the foot of the bed and massaged his calf.

'You know, these power cuts,' she said, 'they always remind me of your mother. Your aunt must be fed up of hearing me say this all the time, but I can't help it. I can't. Nowadays, your mother is the first thing I think of when I wake up and the last thing I think of before I go to sleep.'

Varun didn't say anything. He was surprised Grandma was speaking so openly to him.

She continued. 'There's so much of your father in you, but your hands are hers. See? And so are your fingers. They're long and slender, just like hers. The hands of an engineer, a creator.' She sniffed and wiped her cheeks. 'I'm tired, beta. I'm going to rest. You stay if you want.'

'Okay.'

He listened to her shift in bed and lie down. Poppy whined at being moved, but soon they both settled into a silence interrupted occasionally by Grandma clearing her throat. She was so different from when he and Ma and Pa visited during the holidays. She used to embroider shawls or hand-knit sweaters at the dining table and tell him stories about Ma's childhood. But now she rarely spoke. Her voice had turned brittle, rough yet delicate like those buildings in the place beyond the wall, ready to collapse at the slightest touch. She belonged there, he thought. He knew it was cruel to think that, but she would be more at home there than here.

And what about him?

He massaged his calf muscles. They twisted and writhed under his palms, moving with a life of their own. The candle flame sputtered. Shadows flickered. And then sharpened. He watched in horror as what looked like the shadow of a boy lengthened away from his leg and across the floor. Before he could react, the candle flame died, trailing a column of smoke.

'I... I'll get it, Grandma.'

He patted the ground, terrified that the darkness around him might move.

But the pain in his leg was diminishing. It was as though there was a crack in the base of his heel and all of the pain was seeping out of him and spreading across the floor. He again thought he was urinating, but his trousers were dry. And then it was over. There was no more pain. It was such a relief that he shivered. He relit the candle.

For an instant, he saw movement, a strange shape leaping across the room, but it was only Grandma rolling over in her sleep. It was nothing, he told himself as he inspected his calf. Just a trick of the light, a play of the shadows.

37

Sleep. It's all you do anyway. Sleep and complain and sleep and weep and sleep again. Pathetic. What kind of parent outlives one child and ignores the other? You should've died with your husband. At least then you wouldn't have lived to see the death of your daughter. Remember the silhouette of her body under the shroud? Remember the flesh of her hands turned pale white? That flesh of your own, lighting up with fire. How many days did you smell ash in the house, taste ash in your food?

Sleep. While your grandson, your dead daughter's son, sits only a few feet away from you on the floor.

Old, miserable woman!

All this pain in your bones, in your heart. You are fractured. And the cracks run deep. What are you waiting for? The final hammer blow that will shatter you into a million pieces?

Don't worry.

Soon.

Soon you will be dust scattered to the wind.

38

Zarina was holding Jyoti's hand as Hema spoke.
'The trust has been able to put together enough funds to cover the course fees for one of our teachers. Board and lodging included. Now, there are four major fields of study: environmental protection, human rights, education, and, of course, disability. There's a special module on empowering the blind. Added to that is the fact that the course is run by a group of internationally renowned experts. I'm sure you can appreciate that this is a great opportunity.'

'Yes, ma'am.'

'That does not mean it's a free pass.'

'No, ma'am.'

'This is not a holiday. An application will have to be submitted. I'll take over work on the grant while you focus on this. The entire experience, while extremely rewarding, can be intense. It will require a lot of dedication, hard work, and sacrifice.'

Zarina squeezed Jyoti's hand, and she squeezed back. This was what they'd talked about for so long, this was the opportunity Jyoti had been waiting for. To learn how to bring about sustained and meaningful change.

'How long is the course, ma'am?'

'Six months.'

'It sounds comprehensive.'

'Yes,' Hema said with a sigh, 'but it's in Thiruvananthapuram.'

'What?'

'Now I know that sounds impossible,' Hema said, 'especially considering how circumstances have changed for you. But I still wanted to offer the opportunity to you first. You're the ideal candidate.'

Jyoti let out a hollow laugh. Behind her, in another part of the house, she heard a click, double-click, and click again.

'A leadership course on social change might be the catalyst that will help you, and us, in the broader movement. It's been a decade since you joined us, Jyoti, and you tell me, have things changed as much as we would like? We are still isolated. We are still oppressed. It is still society and social barriers that continue to label and shun us. And people either do not understand or do not care. Where is the education? We need to take matters into our own hands, and you can help us do that.'

Jyoti wished Hema and Zarina had never come. Why dangle this in front of her just to snatch it away?

As though sensing her thoughts, Hema said, 'We've kept you long enough. Thank you for the tea and biscuits. Please think about what I've said.'

'But-'

'You don't have to tell me your answer now. Think about it. And I in turn will reach out to the trust and the organization to find out if there's any way we can make this work. Let's discuss this after your first week back.' Hema took Jyoti's hands in her own. 'I'm sorry to have placed you in such a position. But Jyoti, I'm tired of society telling us what we can and cannot do. I know you feel the same way. Please, think about it.'

'We better hurry, it's going to rain,' Zarina said. She hugged Jyoti, kissed her on the cheek, and whispered, 'Sorry about the ambush. I only found out on the way.'

'You should go instead of me.'

'Yeah, right. I don't know half as much as you do about all this. Oh, before I forget.' She handed over a tiffin container. 'It's not much, just some biryani.'

'You shouldn't have.'

'Shush. Don't look so sad. I'll call you tonight.'

Hema issued instructions to her driver. She said goodbye and Jyoti said the same as car doors banged shut and the engine turned on. Only then did she realize that Hema had thanked her for the biscuits that she herself had brought. The wind picked up. There was a rumble of thunder. Jyoti stepped back inside the house and shut the front door, her thoughts drifting towards Thiruvananthapuram with its high humidity, heavy rainfall, and the sea lapping against its shoreline.

'Jyoti?'

'Yes, Mama. Coming.'

'They're gone?'

'Yes.'

'You look tired.'

'I am tired.'

'How long has it been since you oiled your hair?'

'Why?'

'Looks dull. And unkempt. You should take more care when there are visitors.'

'What do you want me to do, Mama?'

'Why did they drop by?'

Jyoti tapped her shoes with her cane. She decided to throw caution into the wind and told Mama about the opportunity in Thiruvananthapuram. As she spoke, she considered the risk she was taking.

Mama processed this information. 'And this woman wants you to go?'

'Why do you always call her this woman or that woman? I've known her for more than a decade and you've met her hundreds of times. You know her name.'

'Well? She wants you to go?'

'Yes.'

'She's mad.'

'Why?'

'What do you mean, why?'

Jyoti gripped her cane. 'She asked me to think about it.'

'What's there to think about? You have responsibilities here that you can't abandon. She should know that. You have to stay at home now, who else will take care of Varun? Even this current arrangement of you working at the school is unwise. Maybe you should take a break for a year or two, or find some job you can do from home.'

'Mama. Where is this coming from? We talked about this already. What is the point of me staying at home if he's at school?'

'And after school?'

'We'll be done around the same time. I might be an hour or two late sometimes, but that's all.'

'He's just a child. How will he manage without you? What if there's an emergency or he hurts himself and has to be taken to the hospital?'

'You're here.'

'But I'm also unwell, no? I'm also recovering, no? I can't be expected to do everything and-'

'Everything?'

'I thought by now you'd have realized this teaching thing should be put on hold.'

'You haven't helped at all.' Jyoti struggled to keep her voice steady. 'Name one time, just one time since Varun has arrived, that you've lifted a finger to help.'

'What nonsense are you saying? Who flew across the country to take care of Varun? Who had to deal with Alok's money-grubbing relatives? And all that horrible paperwork. And what about the funeral? While you sat here doing nothing. Do you know how much I've sacrificed for you? You're so selfish. So stubborn. No. I forbid it. I forbid you from going to that wretched school again.'

Jyoti tottered. 'You'll stop me, will you?'

'I-'

'And how will you stop me when you can't even get out of bed?'

'Hold your tongue. I'll whip you if you don't mind your place.'

'Oh, I will, Mama. I'll wake up and feed you and clothe you and take care of you. That's what you want, isn't it? A good daughter. A horse you can whip. Thank you, Mama, for this grand life you've given me. Hand and foot I'll serve you till I die.' Blood roared in her ears and she couldn't hear Mama anymore, just muted sounds that slid over her. She staggered out of the room, slamming her shoulder so hard against the edge of the door that she lost her balance.

39

Varun had heard everything. He didn't move till Jyoti Aunty closed the door to her room. He crept back inside his room. He curled a pillow around his head and hummed. He hummed till his throat hurt.

40

Jyoti rubbed her forehead. She was filled with the urge to smash her pottery against the wall, to grind them under her feet into powder. Anything destructive. She wanted it so much that her jaw ached. Instead, she sat on her bed, trying hard not to snap her cane in her hands as she concentrated on her breathing.

The last time she and Mama had fought like this had been over two years ago. She and Anu had planned a trip to Ladakh. They both wanted to explore the area around Leh. Their intention wasn't to hike to Stok Kangri or any of the passes, which required equipment or guides, but to eat local food and try butter tea, visit monasteries and all-women organizations, and learn more about Ladakhi culture and customs. Most of all, she wanted to follow a gentle trail and find a ledge where she could sit in peace and listen to the mountains. But no, Mama had been adamant. *How will you manage? Even with Anu, how on earth will you manage? What next? You'll scale K2?* The weather turned the next week and there were landslides. Vindicated, Mama took every opportunity she got to read aloud newspaper articles on the rising death toll.

The doorbell rang. Jyoti flexed her stiff fingers. It was perfect timing. She went and opened the front door. 'Hello? Who is it?'

'Hi, Jyoti. It's me.'

It really was perfect timing. 'Hi, Praveen.'

'May I come in?'

She tilted her head to the bedrooms behind her but couldn't hear a sound. 'Yes, sure.' He wiped his feet on the welcome mat and stepped inside, his footsteps loud as he followed her to the living room. She flicked on the lights and sat on the divan. He sat next to her, so close that she could smell his aftershave and the cigarette smoke that lingered on him. The smell was not unpleasant.

'You're quiet,' he said after a while. 'Everything okay?'

'I'm fine.'

'Tired?'

'Tired.'

'What's going on?'

'Have you ever been to Thiruvananthapuram?'

'Why? Is that another place we should visit?'

'Have you been?'

'I haven't. But I've been to Kerala twice. I went with some friends to Munnar. That was a lot of fun. It was just after high school and we smoked a lot of hash. I also went with my mother to the Biennale exhibition in Kochi. That was a few years later.'

'Did you like it?'

'I didn't really understand half the art exhibits I saw.'

'No, no. I meant... what did you think of Kerala?'

'Oh. Wet. Muggy. I don't know. Everyone loves Kerala and wants to retire in the backwaters, but not me. See how it gets flooded every year.'

Jyoti was thinking of lush fields, calm estuaries, a collective of like-minded individuals she could learn from.

'Why are you asking about Kerala?' he asked.

'No reason. Simply.'

They sat in silence. Jyoti struggled to pull herself away from the conversation she'd had with Mama. Praveen was restless. He cracked his knuckles. He shifted his weight. He cleared his throat.

'What's wrong?' she asked.

'Nothing. The usual. Did you get my messages?'

'When did you send them?'

'An hour ago?'

'It's been a bit busy over here.'

'Oh yes, how could I forget? It's always a bit busy over here.'

'No need to be so touchy.'

'Who said I was being touchy? I'm not being touchy. I was just asking if you got my messages.'

A few seconds passed before Jyoti asked, 'What did you message me about?'

'Nothing.'

'Nothing?'

'Yeah.'

'You sure you don't want to talk about it? Or I could listen to them now.'

'Forget it.'

'Okay.' She stood up.

'Where are you going?'

'Tea always helps me calm down.' She made her way to the kitchen and started boiling water. She peeled and grated ginger, relieved to have something to do that relied on muscle memory. At last, she heard him sigh and join her.

'I'm sorry. I'm acting like a child when things are so stressful for you,' he said.

'They are. But what to do?'

'I think it's amazing.'

'What is?'

'How you cope. I can't imagine how hard it must be. Even making tea must be-'

'You don't need to say that.'

'No, no, I mean it. It must be such a struggle.'

Jyoti threw a heaped spoonful of sugar into the pot. It was probably a bad idea to tell him he was being patronizing, especially when she was upset and he was moody. She never understood why sighted people felt the need to congratulate her on completing the most mundane of tasks. Even those close to her. Why was the bar set so low?

'My parents,' he said, 'have issued an ultimatum.'

'Oh?'

'One month.'

'And then?'

'If I don't agree to marry someone of their choosing, I'll be thrown out. Disinherited.'

'Uncle and Aunty said that?'

'My father did. Classy guy. How am I supposed to happily marry some stranger? Oh, she's successful. Great. She has some job in equity analysis. Great. She wants to have three children, two boys and a girl, over the next five years. Terrific. Go on, dictate my life, don't worry about what I want. Even my mom is on his side!' He exhaled. 'I just... I don't know what's going to happen and it worries me.'

'I'm sorry.'

'Me too. I shouldn't be unloading on you.'

'Happens.'

'Looks like we won't be going to Havelock after all.'

'No.'

'Maybe we should still go? Sunny beaches? The sea? And I know how to ride a scooter.'

'We'll have to take Varun and my mother with us. Won't that be fun? The three of us riding pillion. One child causing pandemonium, one elderly lady emotionally blackmailing everyone.'

'Let's just ditch them. Let's just ditch everyone in the world.'

She smiled sadly.

'What am I supposed to do, Jyoti?' he said, his voice catching.

She heard him fidgeting with his lighter, igniting a flame. She reached out and squeezed his hand. When he didn't let go, when his thumb roamed the ridges of her knuckles, she felt a cord in her navel tighten. 'Don't smoke so much, man,' she whispered.

'Always taking care of me.'

'Me?'

'Doctor Jyoti. Remember? There was this time when my parents weren't at home and I had come over after school because I was unwell. Fifth standard, I think. You ordered me to lie down. Anuradha had a cassette player with earphones that you'd stolen from her. You pretended the earphones were a stethoscope. You pretended to be my doctor and listened to my heart.'

Jyoti couldn't remember this, but her mind was too preoccupied by the counter between them, her hand in his hand, his thumb tracing her thumb. The tea was bubbling. There was so much pressure building within her. And just when she felt him lean towards her, she heard a bone-crunching thud.

41

Something was wrong. Usha was lying in bed, listening to the low murmur of conversation between Jyoti and her so-called friend. And she was also in a deserted Munirka, watching Anu and Alok enter a crumbling house and be buried alive.

'Oh, oh, oh.' She thumped her chest.

Her calf muscles ached like never before and pressure was building in her bladder. She staggered out of bed and sat down with a huff on the commode. Her forearms glistened with sweat. She shivered, and it took her some time to relax and urinate.

'Oh, what is going on?'

She rubbed her throbbing calf muscles. Why had she said those things to Jyoti? True, it was what she was thinking, but that was no excuse. The patterns in the tiles blurred as she remembered how Varun had come to her bedroom to share his candle. How sweetly he'd checked on Poppy. Without him, Poppy might have passed away.

The ceiling light flickered.

This place was so old. How many times had it been renovated, rewired, repaired? Imagine if it crumbled. And buried her alive.

The lightbulb popped.

Darkness engulfed the bathroom. She wiped herself and was about to wash her hands when her skin prickled and burst into goose pimples. Something had brushed past her.

'Hello?' Her voice was faint. She was being silly. Of course, there was no one there with her in the bathroom. Even though she thought she could see the silhouette of a woman standing in the corner. A woman who looked like Anu.

'I... hello?'

There was an electric hum.

Hello.

Usha gasped. She stumbled back and her elbow hit the wall. She bumped into another wall where the door had been. Her vision swirled with kaleidoscopic patterns in the darkness and she gibbered as she patted surfaces, unable to tell left from right, up from down. She found the door, the door handle, and was about to yank it open and flee when a hand wrapped around her ankle.

Before she could scream, she was falling.

The world swiftly rose up to greet her and her head collided with the edge of the sink. Everything went warm. What had happened? Why was she lying on the bathroom floor? And who was that? Who was in her bathroom, roaring with laughter?

42

Jyoti opened the door to Mama's bedroom and asked, 'What was that sound?'

'She's not in here,' Praveen said, behind her.

She knocked on the bathroom door. 'Mama? Are you okay?' There was no response. 'I'm coming in.' She tried the door but there was a weight leaning against it on the other side. She pushed the door open with her shoulder and squeezed inside the bathroom. She knelt and found legs, arms, shoulders, Mama lying at an awkward angle.

'Um, is aunty okay?' Praveen asked. 'Should I... Oh. Holy shit. Holy shit.'

'Praveen.'

'What happened? What the hell do we do?'

'Praveen. Call an ambulance, please.'

'Okay. Yeah. Right, right. Okay. Which hospital?'

'Republic. It's the closest.'

'Got it.'

Jyoti took a steadying breath. She found her phone in her hand, she'd forgotten it was in her hand, and searched for advice online. The automated voice blared in the bathroom's enclosed space.

CALL YOUR LOCAL EMERGENCY NUMBER.

KEEP THE PERSON STILL.

STOP ANY BLEEDING.
WATCH FOR CHANGES IN BREATHING.
KEEP THE HEAD AND SHOULDERS ELEVATED.

She tenderly tipped Mama on to her back. She folded a towel and slid it under her head.

AVOID MOVING THE PERSON'S NECK.

'Sorry, Mama.'

IF THE PERSON SHOWS NO SIGN OF CIRCULATION, IF THE PERSON IS NOT BREATHING, COUGHING, OR MOVING, BEGIN CPR.

She didn't know CPR. She knelt close to Mama, like they were huddled together in prayer. Praveen was giving directions to someone. The tap was dripping. And there it was. Faint, strained, but a drawing of breath nonetheless.

'Okay.'

She wiped her cheeks. Six, seven times, she wiped her cheeks.

'Okay, Mama, okay.'

There was a smell of urine in the bathroom, and on Mama's behalf she flushed. She knew this smell would live with her till the end of her life. Praveen knocked on the bathroom door and she shifted to block his view.

'They're on their way,' he said.

'Good.'

Her mind was emptying.

'Is there anything we should do?' he asked.

'I don't know.'

'Let's... um, let's think about this. If we're going to the hospital then we need to put together her medical records. Right?'

It was a struggle to follow what he was saying.

'Jyoti! Are you listening to me? Do you know where her medical records are? Or her hospital ID card?'

'Chest of drawers, second from the top. It should be the topmost folder.'

She heard him open and close drawers, rifle through papers.

'Insurance cards,' she murmured. 'Find her insurance cards too.'

'Done. I'm going to open the front gate for them, okay?' he shouted. 'I'll let them in.' He ran out of the room. The front door banged.

She held Mama's hand. For so long Mama had been complaining about a drip in the bathroom ceiling. Maybe she slipped and fell.

'Jyoti Aunty?'

NO! No, no, no, no, no. She shut the bathroom door.

'Jyoti Aunty, is Grandma okay?'

She squeezed out of the bathroom and reached for him, found his hand, and led him away.

'Is Grandma okay?'

'She fell.'

'Is she dead?'

The word was like a kick to the chest. She took him to his bedroom and smoothed the hair from his forehead. 'No, she's not dead, but a fall at her age can be serious. We'll have to take her to the hospital.'

'Should I carry anything with me?'

'What? Where?'

'To the hospital.'

'Oh, I didn't mean…'

The poor boy had seen Anu and Alok turn to ash. She didn't want him to sit beside Mama in an ambulance, or wait for hours in a hospital. But what could she do? She couldn't just leave him alone at home. Outside, a vehicle rumbled down the driveway and crunched to a halt. Footsteps thudded through the house and Praveen was shouting about where Mama was. Two men discussed how to stretcher Mama out. There was no time. She needed help.

'Praveen,' she called out.

'Come on, Jyoti, let's go. My bike's parked outside. They're taking your mother.'

'I need you to do me a favour.'

'What? Sure. Tell me, anything.'

'Someone has to stay with Varun. Can you do that, please. Just stay here with him? I'll call my neighbour, Mrs Naronha. She'll come over in ten minutes. I'll call my friend Zarina too. She might take a bit longer, but after one of them gets here, you can leave.'

'What are you saying? You don't want me to come with you?'

'Someone has to stay with Varun.'

'Let's just take him.'

'No.'

'What's the big deal? He can wait with us.'

'He's too young. I don't... I don't know what's going to happen.'

'But how will you manage by yourself?'

'I'll manage.'

'Are you sure?'

'Watch him till Mrs Naronha or Zarina come over. Please. Do this for me, okay?'

'I'll watch him all night, it's no big deal. I'm more worried about you.'

'I'll be fine.' She filled a bottle of water, checked her

handbag for her wallet, phone, keys, and Mama's hospital records. She crammed the insurance cards in as well. 'There's food in the kitchen. Biryani. He normally eats around this time. Try to keep him calm. Bed at eight.' She grabbed her cane and sweater.

'Jyoti…' He caught her hand. He squeezed, unknowingly hurting her swollen wrist. 'Call me if you need help.'

The two ambulance men were moving through the house. They shuffled as they carried Mama out on a stretcher.

'I need to go.'

'Jyoti Aunty?'

She found Varun standing in the hallway by the front door and knelt to speak to him. 'I'll be back soon. You stay here, okay? This uncle is going to be here if you need anything, and Aunty Zarina will be here soon as well.'

'I can come.'

'I know. But I want you to stay here. I'll be back soon.'

'When?'

'Soon.'

'Promise?'

'God promise.'

What if she was wrong? What if she was so wrong? She shouldn't make promises she couldn't keep, but there was no time to second-guess herself. She kissed him on the forehead and hugged him.

'Be good, okay? Please.'

She pressed his little hands between her own, tried to convince herself that everything would be okay and that this wasn't a foolish decision, then hurried after the men and Mama.

43

Praveen lingered by the gate, watching traffic till the sky shivered with the first few flashes of lightning. He walked back to the bungalow. His mother would be leaning against the balcony railing and peering down the road, her face pinched with worry. At least he had an excuse for staying away from home. Maybe his father would even be distracted by someone else's tragedy and take a break from issuing threats and micro-managing his life.

It was quiet inside the bungalow. Strange that only a few minutes ago there'd been such chaos. The hallway walls were stained from Jyoti sliding her palms across their surfaces to guide herself throughout the house. Why hadn't they installed a railing? Wouldn't that have made it easier for her? He inspected the bathroom and found a smear of blood on the floor tiles. Water dripped from the ceiling. It wasn't hard to imagine the old lady slipping and cracking her head. At her age, who knew how bad it could be? His uncle had passed away in his fifties after falling down a flight of stairs.

The ceiling light flickered.

It was one of those fluorescent tube lights, its casing cluttered with the bodies of dead moths. He squinted at the fixture, the peeling flakes of paint, and the rings of mould. This house was old. They should just sell the property and be done with the damned place. The location would fetch them a terrific amount of money, and they could easily relocate. Escape. Begin again.

The ceiling light popped.

Darkness engulfed the bathroom. He stumbled. He collided against the commode and pain exploded in his knee. He yanked open the door with a curse.

Sitting on the old lady's bed, he massaged his kneecap. There were tangles of hair on the sheets and he considered tidying the bed when he noticed a stray dog lying within the folds of the blanket. But no, this wasn't a stray. This was the mutt the old woman had adopted some hundred years ago. He stroked its back. The dog blinked. Its eyes were glazed over, covered in a glossy film, and it seemed incapable of lifting its head. He poked it hard in the ribs. The dog closed its eyes.

What the hell was going on here?

He left the room to check on the boy. Even though he'd smashed his knee against the commode, his calf muscles were killing him now. In the hallway, he stubbed his toe against a chest of drawers. The pain was maddening. It was infuriating.

A drink would help.

Yes, a drink would help. Jyoti kept a bottle of gin in her room for emergencies when her mother drove her nuts, and he found it and poured himself a hefty amount. He sipped at his drink. Would they have reached the hospital by now? Bangalore traffic did not yield to ambulance sirens. He wondered how many died in transit.

It's true. The old lady might already be dead.

Don't say that.

Why not?

Because hadn't Jyoti suffered enough? She'd lost her sister, she didn't need to lose her mother. And he knew it was selfish, but he worried that another tragedy in her life might push her further away from him.

What if the opposite happened?

Meaning?

What if the old lady's death brought Jyoti closer to you?

But that's not what happened after Anuradha and her husband died. They'd gone from talking every night to barely seeing each other. And she'd retreated into herself. There was her mother to care for, the boy, too many bloody responsibilities, and not enough time to meet or talk.

Yes, but if the old lady died, then maybe Jyoti would recognize you for who you are. Someone who will care for her and protect her. Not a man like your father, but a real man. A good man. The man who will save her from her own life.

Maybe.

There would be no more pressure from your father.

Yeah, right. He'd be the first to object. A blind woman? With a child?

But there'd be all the money in the world from the sale of this property.

Huh. That's true.

Imagine it.

What?

Imagine if the old lady died.

For a moment, he did. He did imagine it.

There. Nothing wrong with that. No harm.

No. He and Jyoti could relocate to another part of the city. Or maybe to another part of the country. Back to Bombay, even. She wouldn't need to go to that school anymore. She could stay at home while he set up a business.

You could take care of her, and she could take care of you.
But there was the boy.
Well, imagine if the boy was gone as well.
Gone? Gone where?
Imagine it.
How could he imagine that, for heaven's sake? That was too much.
Haven't you already?
The pain in his calf muscles flared. It rose. It grasped at his shoulders, his neck, like some enormous being wrapping its arms around him and crushing him. Praveen poured himself another drink. He took a long sip. He chewed his ice cubes. And yes, he allowed himself to imagine this as well.

44

The ambulance was a cramped tempo. One man drove while the other sat next to Mama and monitored her vitals. Jyoti tried to take up as little space as possible.

She dialled Mrs Naronha.

The line didn't connect.

She dialled again.

An automated voice stated that the number she was dialling no longer existed.

She dialled again.

An automated voice apologized and asked her to try again later.

She remembered Mama mentioning the rains had knocked out Mrs Naronha's telephone connection. She called their old neighbour Mr Shah, but he was out of town. She didn't have the phone numbers of Mama's other friends, and she'd left Mama's phone at home. How stupid. How unbelievably stupid.

She called Zarina.

'Hi.'

'Listen, I'm going to Republic, my mother-'

'What? This -nection is -rrible.'

'I'm going to Republic Hospital. My mother hurt herself.'

'Oh no! -at happened?'

'I don't know. I think she slipped and fell in the bathroom. I've left Varun at home with a friend. Can you go over to my place and stay with him?'

'What? Varun?'

'Can you go to my place and watch over Varun?'

'-re do you want -o go?'

'I'm going to Republic. You go to my place.'

'I'm on my way.'

Jyoti hung up. The ambulance was crawling through traffic. It was hard to think with the siren blaring and cars all around them beeping relentlessly. She held Mama's hand, which was limp and cold.

'Don't do this to me, Mama.'

Look. This is your apartment in Bombay. The living room is bare and the walls are white, but you and Jyoti will purchase a carpet of the deepest blue. Like the ocean, you will say, reminding her of her childhood paper boats. You both will pretend to swim in its depths.

Look. This is your bedroom. There is no bed, but you and Jyoti will purchase a new one so large you will call it your own country. The sheets will be clean, crisp, tucked in at the corners, and fresh with the scent of detergent.

Look. This is your life. Every night you and Jyoti will lie next to each other and believe you are building a future together, brick by brick. The money you earn will support you both. She will not need to work. She will be grateful that you have given her the life she deserves. She will be grateful that you are her man, and she is your woman.

Look. A boy is coming. He will take from you everything you hold dear.

46

When the two men carried Grandma out of the house, Varun had glimpsed the crescent whites of her eyes. He didn't know how, but he knew he'd done this. It was his fault. Jyoti Aunty too must have thought this, because why else would she leave him behind?

He heard the murmur of voices from the living room. Had she already returned? Maybe Grandma was okay, maybe the doctors had checked her and said everything was fine. But when he stepped out of his room, he found the house was dark. Uncle Praveen was slumped in a chair in the living room, sipping a drink, and crunching ice cubes. There was a sharp smell in the air, reminding Varun of times when guests visited and Pa twisted open bottles he wasn't allowed to touch.

He took a step back towards his room when Uncle Praveen spoke.

'Hello, little boy. Can't relax?'

He shook his head.

'Same. Are you hungry?'

He shook his head again.

'Same. Come, sit with me. Let's talk.'

The floors were cold, and he shivered as he crossed the room and took a seat.

'Are you worried about your grandmother?'

He nodded.

'Well, your aunty hasn't called with any news, but no news might be good news. Let's stay positive.'

'Pa used to say that.'

'What?'

'Let's stay positive. Or no, let's be positive. He used to say that whenever I needed a blood test. Because my blood type is B+.'

'Funnily enough, I understood that joke.' Even though Uncle Praveen's voice remained rough as sandpaper, he spoke in a softer tone. 'I'm sorry about what happened to your parents. I knew your mother. From a long time ago when she and I were your age. Your mother and your aunty and I used to play together in the back garden. Hide-and-seek or cops-and-robbers. For some reason they always made me the robber. But we lost touch. After your aunty lost her sight and I changed schools, I didn't meet them so often. That happens, you know, especially in this city. People lose touch. Anyway, your aunty liked telling me about your parents. What they were up to. What you were up to. It's such a shame. To have died so young.'

Varun pulled his knees up to his chest.

'Oh. Sorry.' Uncle Praveen drained his glass, coughed, and wiped his chin. 'You know, I was just dreaming about them. Isn't that funny? I've not seen Anuradha in decades and I've never even met your father, but I had this intense vision of them. You were with them. The three of you in a colony. Living in peace in Delhi.'

'A colony?'

'Doesn't that sound nice?'

Varun didn't say anything.

'Your family, still alive. You, still living with them. Maybe your grandmother visiting you all so that your aunty and I have the house to ourselves. The city to ourselves, why not? We could go wherever we wanted without looking over our shoulders. We wouldn't have to behave in this secret-secret way anymore. My god, we would be free.'

'Free?'

'Do you understand what I mean?'

Varun shook his head.

'Just imagine if your mummy and daddy were at home and one of your relatives turned up. A child who is now parentless, homeless. What would your parents do? They would have no choice but to help, right? They're not monsters. But then, what happens to their lives? What happens to your life?' He snapped his fingers. 'Gone. Poof. Vanished. Just like that it changes. Now there's one more person in the house to feed, one more person to dress, one more person to care for. Now there's no more time with your mummy and daddy because your mummy and daddy are too busy paying attention to this other person. What do you do?' He was slurring his words. 'Tell me, what do you do?'

'Uncle...'

'Yes? Speak up.'

'Why are you telling me this?'

'Because... because I just want things to be the way they were before. Is that so bad? Huh? Your parents would still be alive. You would be in Delhi. And Jyoti and I... well, things wouldn't be like how they are now. Your poor aunty. How she has suffered since you moved in. Do you even know?'

Varun hugged his knees.

'You don't know. How could you? You're just a child. A

little boy.' Uncle Praveen tried to drink from his glass but it was empty and slipped from his hand. It landed on the carpet with a muffled thud. 'Poor Jyoti. She's lost so much. We've lost so much. Wouldn't it be nice if we could at least have our lives back?'

'Uncle?'

'Hmm?'

'I don't understand. What do you mean, if you could have your lives back?'

'Think. It's obvious, no?'

'Do you want me to go? Does Jyoti Aunty want me to go?'

Uncle Praveen closed his eyes.

'Did Jyoti Aunty say that?'

'Yes,' Uncle Praveen whispered, before he fell asleep.

Varun stood up. His body felt strange and heavy, like it wasn't his own. He wanted to call Jyoti Aunty, hear her voice, but he couldn't find her number and instead dialled those digits he knew by heart.

'Hello?' a girl answered.

He could see her holding the phone to her ear, her lips so close to the receiver that her words crackled with static.

'I know it's you,' Komal said.

He could see her living room, the dining table, and the circular jute placemats.

'My parents got caller ID. Can you hear me?'

He could see the sofa where Ma and aunty sat down with their steaming cups of coffee to talk.

'Why won't you say something?'

In the background, aunty was asking her who was calling.

'If you aren't going to say anything, then don't call. Okay?'

Aunty was asking if it was him.

'Don't call again. Ever.'

He remembered how she hugged him the day after the accident. How when she let go, his shirt was damp with her tears.

'You promised,' Komal said, her voice catching.

He whispered, 'I'm sorry,' just as the line went dead.

He gently placed the receiver down.

He went to Jyoti Aunty's room. He touched her music player. He touched the clay figurines on her shelves. On her table, he found a strange stencil that had the letters of the alphabet and their corresponding patterns of raised dots. It was for learning braille. Not sure if he was doing it correctly, he wrote a letter to her using the tip of a pencil to poke holes in the back of a page. He brushed his fingertips across the letters and remembered Jyoti Aunty telling him she'd struggled to learn braille. He wrote in English as well, just in case. After he was done, he slid his torch inside his pocket. There was no need for anything else. Jyoti Aunty had made him promise to be good, and if she wanted him gone, then wasn't this being good?

She had made the same promise to him that Ma had made.

Resisting the urge to crawl under her blanket and wait for her, he left the room. Still in his t-shirt and pyjamas, he unlocked the front door and slipped out into the night. The note he'd written lay on her bed, held in place by Pa's coin.

⠛⠕⠕⠙⠃⠽⠑ ⠚⠽⠕⠞⠊ ⠁⠥⠝⠞⠽ ⠊ ⠺⠊⠇⠇ ⠍⠊⠎⠎ ⠽⠕⠥ ⠊ ⠓⠁⠧⠑ ⠛⠕⠝⠑ ⠞⠕ ⠃⠑ ⠺⠊⠞⠓ ⠍⠽ ⠏⠁⠗⠑⠝⠞⠎

Goodbye, Jyoti Aunty. I will miss you. I have gone to be with my parents.

47

The doctor on call stitched the cut in Mama's head. Jyoti heard him snip the thread, wheel away from the cot, and unsnap his latex gloves. He moved with a young man's impatience. He instructed a nurse to apply a bandage and collect some blood before striding away to check on the next patient in the emergency room. The nurse came around the side of the cot and tore open plastic wrappings. As she worked, she asked Jyoti what she did for a living, where was her home, and whether she'd come alone. She offered to help Jyoti with the forms and payment, and Jyoti accepted. This late in the evening there were few provisions in place for the visually impaired. The nurse's name was Soorya. She had a four-year-old daughter who she hoped would grow up to look after her the way Jyoti was looking after her mother. Soorya filled in the paperwork. She also gave Jyoti a paper cup of hot tea. Jyoti mumbled her thanks. She wanted to tell Soorya that she was, like the tea she'd offered, incredibly sweet, but Soorya was called away.

There were other patients in the emergency room. An old man complained about how long he'd been waiting to receive treatment. His petulance made Jyoti want to cry.

'Oh... where am I?' Mama said.

Jyoti grabbed her hand. She held it against her cheek, her

forehead. 'You're in the emergency room at Republic, Mama.'

'My head.'

'They had to give you stitches.'

'Stitches?'

'Nine stitches. It was a deep cut. They had to shave a patch of your hair.'

'Oh...' she groaned.

'Does anything else hurt?'

'No. But my head is killing me.'

She kissed Mama's knuckles and suddenly she was so angry that she wanted to scream at Mama, tell her that she was old, that she was frail, that she needed to be careful for heaven's sake, and why was she behaving like an irresponsible child. 'What... what happened? We found you on the bathroom floor. Did you faint? The doctor is worried it might be something serious like a blood clot.'

'No. I didn't faint. Nothing like that. I... I slipped. That's all.' She sounded uncertain.

'You can't remember what happened?'

'I just said, no?'

'Okay, Mama.'

'Blood clot... what nonsense.'

'They said maybe a blood clot. It's pretty common for people your age. Or it could've been low blood pressure. Or something else entirely. They were trying to rule out some of the more serious possibilities. They didn't know.'

'They never know. All these doctors.'

'You were unconscious, Mama.'

'I slipped, that's all. Water has been dripping from that wretched crack in the ceiling for years now and I've been telling you we need to get it fixed. The bulb died, I couldn't see, I slipped. Nothing else. Such a big reaction. And what do you mean, people your age?'

'Never mind. Just keep calm, Mama. It doesn't matter now.'

'Acting like I'm a hundred years old.'

'Fine. Fine.'

'There was water on the floor.'

'Enough.'

They sat in silence for a while. But when she let go of Mama's hand to reach for her phone, Mama said, 'Forget it.'

'Forget what?'

'Forget what I said this evening. I don't know why I said it and I know I shouldn't have said it, and now let's forget it and not break our heads over it.'

Jyoti supposed this was an apology. 'You're the one trying to break your head.'

'Very funny. We'll figure it out, okay?'

'Just help me with the lawyer stuff.'

'I said we'll figure it out, no?'

'Okay, Mama. And I'm sorry, too.'

'Where's Varun?'

'At home. I left him with my friend and Zarina.'

'You left him alone?'

'I told you, I left him with my friend and Zarina.'

'Which friend? That Praveen boy?'

'I didn't want Varun with me in the ambulance. I didn't want him to see you in such a state. Not after everything he's been through.'

The doctor joined them before Mama could respond. He asked her the same questions Jyoti had asked and Mama responded irritably. He checked her response to light. He took her blood pressure. Eventually, he said it was safe to discharge her. But they needed to be careful. No strenuous activity. Someone would have to watch her for the next twenty-four hours. And they'd have to come back tomorrow to collect their test results to see if there were any serious underlying causes.

Jyoti was relieved. They could go home. She didn't even mind Mama muttering that she wasn't some farm animal that needed to be shepherded. She was already thinking about getting back. Varun might still be awake. Hopefully, he'd eaten. Hopefully, he wasn't too worried. She took out her phone and tried to dial Zarina, but was surprised to discover the battery was dead. When had that happened? In all of the commotion, she hadn't heard the phone warn her that the battery was running low. She clicked the power button a few times, hoping it might turn on. Perhaps Soorya had a spare charger or would let her use her phone. She went in search of her, but she hadn't gone very far before she heard someone breathlessly call her name. Zarina grabbed her shoulder and pulled her into a hug.

'Hi,' Zarina said, kissing her cheek. 'How's your mom?'
'What're you doing here?'
'What do you mean? You told me to come to Republic.'
'No! No, I said to go to my place.'
'Your place?'
'Varun is at home. I wanted you to keep an eye on him.'
'He's alone?'
'I left him with someone, but I wanted you there with him as well.'
'Oh. I'm sorry, the connection was so bad, I swear I thought you told me to come to Republic.'

'I didn't!'

'Sorry, sorry. Do you want me to go there now? How's your mom?'

'Give me your phone.'

Jyoti dialled the landline at home. At least she could speak with Varun, let him know everything was okay, and that they'd be back home soon. But no one answered. The line continued to ring and ring till it automatically disconnected. She called again. And again. No luck. Why was no one answering? Unless the calls weren't going through. Surely the rains hadn't knocked out everyone's connections.

She tried Praveen. He didn't answer. She huffed. Why on earth was she having so many problems with phones this night? She dialled again. He didn't answer, and this time she felt a prickle of uneasiness. She dialled and misdialled and dialled again and again till her mind started imagining such frightful possibilities that she headed towards the exit, stopped, turned back, ran into Zarina, and nearly fell to the floor. The phone was still ringing on the other end of the line.

'Are you okay?' Soorya asked, her footsteps hurrying over.

'What happened?' Zarina asked.

'I'm fine,' Jyoti said, clutching Soorya's arm. 'Can we... can we go, please?'

'The doctor has discharged your mother. It's no problem. You can go home.'

'Thank you.' Jyoti wanted to say more but there was no time.

'What's going on?' Zarina asked.

Jyoti was thinking about Hema's words and how untrue they were and how she was such an idiot to have left Varun.

'What's the matter with you?' she heard Mama ask from her cot. 'And what's she doing here? I thought she was watching Varun.'

'Come on, Mama. It's time to go home. Zarina, can you please collect the prescription sheet and get your car? We need to go. Now.'

48

Anu waited by the window. The parking lot was empty, quiet. No sign of Varun. She was about to turn away when she caught sight of a plant pot, its base cracked open and spilling dry soil. There was a flicker of colour. Papa had inspected the same pot when he'd last visited, offering to buy a new one from the market or transplant the raat ki rani to the flowerbeds. *This queen is growing so fast*, he'd said with concern, tenderly lifting its drooping leaves. She'd told him that Alok would complain for weeks if they threw away a pot just because it was broken, and then she'd laughed till her stomach ached when Papa shook his head and said with such disdain, *That husband of yours*.

Alok joined her in the living room. He still hadn't spoken to her after she allowed Varun to leave, only glowering at her whenever she checked on him. Without meaning to, she smirked. He was always such a serious fellow. But her smile faded when she noticed his expression.

'What's the matter?'

'He's coming,' Alok said, eyes ablaze with excitement.

She whirled around and peered through the window, expecting to see Varun standing outside and knocking on the front door. Her yearning was so strong that she felt dizzy. She could sense Varun picking his way towards them. He hadn't yet crossed over but was close.

'What's happened?'

'Couldn't you tell he was coming?' Alok asked.

'I... no. Not till you told me.'

'You couldn't tell.'

She huffed. It was always his way to goad her by first asking a question and then following it up with the same question rephrased as a statement. At least in this place, they were still the same. To some degree.

'Things have to be perfect this time,' he said, 'it's our last chance.'

'But what about Varun?'

'I said he's on his way here.'

'No. What happens after?'

'What do you mean, what happens after?' Alok's eyes narrowed. His voice carried an edge when he spoke. 'Anuradha. We've talked about this. If we do things right, then he stays here with us. We'll be together again as a family. That's what we want. Right?'

'Yes.'

'That's what he needs. Right?'

'Yes.'

'Yes, but?'

'Nothing.'

'Are you sure?'

'Yes.'

'Good. Then let's not talk about this anymore.'

She left him standing in the living room shaking his head, and went to her office. The gramophone was on the floor and she carefully picked it up and placed it on her table. What fun they'd had crafting it together. It had been such a strange, fulfilling joy watching Varun learn to build, like revisiting her own childhood through the eyes of Mama and Papa.

She ran a finger across the table's dusty surface. Everything was the same here, yet so different. When she and Alok first found themselves back in this house, it was the dreams that kept them going. Dreams of Varun.

But something had changed. She'd opened the door for Varun, and he'd opened a door for her. She didn't know how, but now her dreams were replaced by memories, little seeds that bloomed into life.

Like crouching in the mud with Papa and caressing the shoots of a pea plant.

Like sitting on the carpet in the old bungalow and relishing Mama brutally massaging oil into her scalp.

Like coming up with a secret language with Jo while Mama and Papa slept.

Like walking with Jo to school, arms interlinked, their contempt for boys sharp.

Like going on her first date with Alok, the oaf, who wanted to see Agrasen Ki Baoli but changed his mind midway because of the crowds. He'd taken her to a food stall instead and they'd devoured hundreds of pani puris. Or as he insisted on calling them, gol gappas.

Something had happened. She'd stepped through the door Varun had opened and was experiencing her life again in flashes, rich and vibrant, cutting her to ribbons. Mama, Papa, Jo. How could she have forgotten them? These were the lives that had built her own.

She felt a flush of shame for laughing at Alok imitating Jo. Who had she become to act in such a way? No wonder

Varun had left. But now he was coming back. What had happened to make him come back? She imagined him sitting cross-legged on the living-room carpet, laughing and bringing colour and light to this place, and her yearning once again grew so intense that she was dizzy. The feeling swiftly turned to panic at the sight of her table, the line trailing through the dust. What would happen to him if he came back here for good?

She smoothed the curling edge of the cardboard gramophone and remembered Varun leaning forward to listen. It was an act of pure expectation. How he'd looked at her, eyes wide with shock and delight when he caught the scratchy strains of music, like she'd shared with him the world's greatest secret.

Surrounded by piles of paper, tools, and glinting coils of wire, Anu allowed the pieces of her life to slowly return to her. As they did, as memories brought with them familiar joys and complex pains, she knew that every step Varun took towards the colony brought her a step closer to another door and another decision. There wasn't much time.

49

Varun walked through the grove. It was the first time he'd been outside so late in the night, and though the moon was snuffed out, the neighbouring buildings radiated a pale white light. He could see inside several apartments, each the same yet so different. In one, the flicker of a television screen casting shadows, in another, an old man in a vest shuffling past the balcony. A man washing dishes, a woman smoking a cigarette by an open window. There was little movement in the last apartment he saw, just the twitch of curtains.

He wished there was someone with him to hold his hand. Or Poppy to keep him safe.

Gripping the torch, he followed its light. Tree trunks gleamed and then melted into the darkness. Branches whispered. Leaves turned to mulch under his shoes. Varun was so spooked by the restless energy of the grove that he stopped to urinate, but even after he was done there remained an urge to sprint back to the safety of the bungalow.

Where Uncle Praveen lay slumped in the living room.

Varun was shivering by the time he arrived at the boundary wall. Its shards of glass glinted green and amber, and above were clouds and a few dull stars scattered across the sky. The stars did not move out of alignment as he climbed through the hole in the wall. There was no noticeable difference in the air, no sign that he'd crossed from Bangalore to Delhi, but Varun felt like his companions' warning had at last come true.

He was lost.

Keeping the torch in front of him, he headed towards the colony. He didn't run past the pavilion because to do so would be to lose control, to panic, to risk setting free the dangers that lay in wait. He stepped out of the courtyard, ignored the park, crossed the road, and followed the colony's meandering path, wincing whenever he scraped grit or dislodged rubble and the sounds echoed around him.

'I'm sorry,' he whispered, thinking of the stick and the coin. At least the coin would stay with Jyoti Aunty. Who knew where he'd lost the stick? Maybe he and his companions would be reunited in this place. It was, after all, a place where things once lost were found again.

The darkness beyond his beam of light was absolute. He walked past the parking lot where he and Komal and his friends used to play seven stones. The end of the lane was lit up by warm yellow light. The only light in the colony of shadows. It was hard then, to control his body. The closer he got to the house, the more he felt as though the darkness behind him was solidifying, turning to concrete, trapping him in here forever.

He willed himself not to turn back. He knocked on the door. The sound was so loud in the emptiness of the colony that he clenched his toes in his shoes and then thumped the door with the palm of his hand and kicked it so hard that it shuddered in its frame. He cried out, 'It's me, it's me, Ma, it's me, let me in!'

There was a rush of footsteps, the clack of the lock, and

then the door swung open and it was Ma, gaping at him as her shawl slid from her shoulders to the floor. Varun hugged her. He wanted to be lifted into her arms even though he knew he was too old for that.

'Oh, beta,' she said. 'What happened?'

'They don't want me, Ma.'

'Who?'

'He told me. They want me to leave them alone.'

'Who told you?'

'He said Jyoti Aunty has been suffering because of me.'

'What?'

Pa emerged from the shadows of the hallway. 'That's terrible. Whoever this fool is, he has no idea who you are. He shouldn't be saying such things. The truth is, they don't know you and they don't appreciate you. They never did. But we do. We're your family.'

Varun's throat was painfully tight. He looked up at Pa, who was nodding and smiling at him in a reassuring way. Ma was frowning.

'Stay with us,' Pa said. 'Come inside. It's nice and warm.'

This was why he'd come. He knew. But it was still hard not to flinch when the door clicked shut behind him.

'Come,' Pa said, ushering him into the living room.

Varun sat cross-legged on the carpet. Resting on the coffee table was the gramophone he and Ma had made, the battery standing upright and waiting to be connected to the motor. He touched the disc. Its waxy black surface gleamed like it was spinning. He was relieved it wasn't. He didn't want to hear those ghostly voices anymore.

'I brought that out for you,' Pa said. 'You can play a record if you want.'

'I don't understand.'

'What, beta?'

'Why do they want me gone? What did I do? I... I promised to be good.'

Pa was about to say something but Ma held up her hand. She knelt in front of Varun. Her voice was not false or cheery like Pa's when she spoke.

'Who said this?' she asked.

'Jyoti Aunty's friend.'

'Her friend?'

'Uncle Praveen.'

'What did he say? Did he shout at you?'

'He said... he said he and Jyoti Aunty wanted their lives back.'

Ma's face tightened. 'Right. Some man, some idiot said this nonsense to you. Did Jyoti Aunty?'

'No.'

'Then?'

'But he said-'

'Listen to me. People say stupid things when they're scared. They shout and scream. They lie. They break things. They do everything they can to hurt you even though they know what they're saying or doing is wrong. It's childish. And it's not because they mean it but because they're frightened and it's so much easier to turn to anger and lash out.'

'What're you doing?' Pa asked.

She kept her eyes on Varun.

'You didn't see him, Ma. He wasn't shouting. He wasn't breaking anything.'

'That doesn't mean he wasn't scared or angry.'

Varun pulled at the carpet fibres.

Pa put a hand on Ma's shoulder. 'Your mother's just being-'

'When your aunt lost her vision,' Ma said, 'she stopped playing with me in the grove. In fact, she stopped doing a lot of things. She stopped going to school, meeting friends, changing her clothes, taking baths, even getting out of bed. She didn't scream or shout or beat her cane against the walls, but she was obviously scared. Poor Jo. Can you understand, beta? I wish I could go back in time and do it all differently. Back then I thought your grandma had Jo's best interests at heart and was right to force her to stay at home, right to force her not to do this, not to do that, to sit still and obey her every instruction because it was for her own good. I was wrong, of course. Your grandma was just as scared and angry as Jo. There was plenty we could've done, but it took us a long time to learn that, just as it took Jo a long time to accept what was happening.'

Varun pictured Uncle Praveen in the living room, sipping his drink. He seemed so nice when he spoke with Jyoti Aunty.

'Trust me,' Ma said, 'this man will feel bad. One way or the other, he will come to regret what he said.'

Varun could tell she was still angry by the way she tugged her shawl. She sounded more like herself. Her anger made him feel calm, safe even. Despite everything that had happened, he yawned. It was a body-shuddering yawn and he could feel sleep steal over his body. His head drooped.

'You're tired,' Ma said.

'I'm awake.'

'Are you sure you don't want to go back to-'

'Bed,' Pa said.

'I'm awake.'

But he was suddenly so tired. Pa lifted him and carried him

to his room. Ma nudged Pa out of the way and tucked him under the blanket. She combed his hair with her fingertips. He caught a glimpse of his painting hanging above him, Sitana ponticeriana, before he closed his eyes and whispered, 'Goodnight.'

50

Poppy could hear the man outside, the one who'd mistreated her. He was pushing against the windows, testing them to see if they unlatched. In his hands was a plastic bag.

I am here, little digger.

She scuffed the bedsheets.

And when I catch you, the light in your eyes will be MINE.

A door banged against its frame.

She started awake. It took her time to focus. The vet had forced her to swallow medicines and now her mind was dull, her bones turned to liquid. The bed was empty. Where was her ma? She sniffed the air and adrenaline blazed through her body as though a cat had leapt from out of the darkness to claw her face. She crawled to the side of the bed, fell, ignored the pain in her legs, and crawled to the bathroom. Her ma. Her poor ma. Something terrible had happened. The smell of blood was so potent that Poppy tucked her tail between her legs. And there was something else that made her back out of the room and into the hallway.

There wasn't just the smell of blood. There was also the smell of the tunnel, like burnt metal and wisps of black smoke. Something had come through. It was here. He was here. The man with the plastic bag.

Poppy nearly whined again when she noticed someone sitting in the living room. She went stock-still. The fur on her back stood on end, thick and sharp as thorns. She bared her teeth. This man was her sister's friend, but right now he reeked of the tunnel and sharp chemicals that stung her nose. His eyes were closed, his breathing shallow, and for a moment she contemplated leaping at his throat and tearing the life out of him.

But then a door banged again.

She tensed.

He didn't stir.

The front door was swinging on its hinges. Why was it open? What had happened to her ma and her sister? To the boy? She didn't know the answer to the first two, but she had a hunch about the third.

Staying low, she crept past the living room and down the hallway to the front door. Outside, her suspicions were confirmed. There was a strong breeze whipping through the trees, but the trails remained strong. Some men, her ma, and her sister had gone towards the driveway. There were tyre tracks. They must have climbed into a car.

The other trail went in the opposite direction. It was laced with the smell of bitter orange rinds. He'd come full circle, the boy. He was ripe with grief. Something had crossed over from the other side of the tunnel and worked its mischief in the house to lure him away. What promises had it made? Would it ever let him go, or was he vanished from this earth?

It came upon her then, sudden and bright, the wish that she'd had pups. Her ma had denied her that possibility, she knew, but she didn't begrudge her for it. After she and her siblings tore through the plastic bag, after she was rescued and before she was neutered, she had suppressed her instinct and steered clear of other strays. Why would she want pups in a world where men beat dogs, stoned them, tortured them, drove over them, or drowned them? But now she wished for the chance. To see pups climb over each other in their eagerness to be with her. To see their glossy coats catch the light. To lick clean their eyes and teach them canine laws and the invisible territories marked by scent. To feel them draw milk. She wanted that understanding. She wanted to see the promise of their newly formed bones.

Poppy gathered what strength remained in her body and followed the boy's trail.

51

His phone rang and rang and rang. Praveen cursed. His head was throbbing. There was a half-empty glass of water on the coffee table and he gulped it down before reaching for his phone. It was an unknown number. Probably a damned telemarketer. He answered just in time to hear the other person hang up. Perfect. He dropped his phone on the coffee table with a clatter. God, why did he drink so much? He belched and was repulsed by the horrendous taste of stomach acid. He rushed to throw up in the bathroom, then staggered to the kitchen where he rinsed his face under cold water. In the fridge was a tiffin box of biryani, and it was only after he ate more than half of it that his legs stopped trembling and he felt a bit more alive.

All he wanted was to sleep. But he supposed it was probably for the best if he checked on the boy. The boy. His pulse picked up. Had he spoken to the boy while drunk? The things he'd said! But no, no, he was imagining it. He never said those things. Even as he tried to convince himself of what the truth was, he found the front door wide open.

'Varun?' he asked the empty hallway.

'Varun?' he asked the empty rooms of the house.

He raced out, because where else could the bloody boy have gone? Just then a car came hurtling down the driveway.

He was bathed in the glare of its headlights. Something lifted from his body, an awful pain eased up, and for an instant, he thought he saw the shadow of a man flit away, around the house and towards the grove. Standing there, wild-eyed, waiting for whoever it was in the car to come out, Praveen knew the numerous futures he'd imagined with Jyoti were now rapidly coalescing into one.

52

Jyoti unclicked her seatbelt and climbed out of the car the moment Zarina switched off the engine. 'Help my mother inside, will you?' she said. 'I need to check on Varun.' She hurried towards the house. As she fumbled for the keys with one hand, her cane struck something and she stopped. There was someone standing right in front of her.

'Varun?'

'It's me.'

'Praveen!' Her relief was overwhelming. If he was here, then everything was okay, Varun was probably asleep. 'Why didn't you answer my calls?'

'I'm very sorry. I was busy.'

'Busy? With what? I called like a thousand times.'

'There was something related to my previous start-up which I needed to handle.'

'Now?'

'That's the thing with having your own business, the work never ends.'

'I thought your start-up had dissolved.'

'Your mother's okay? What happened to her?'

'She needed stitches, she's fine.'

'That's good, very good. And who's that with her?'

'My friend.'

'Good. Good, good, good. All good.'

Jyoti frowned. Praveen was slurring his words. Worse, his breath smelled sharp and unpleasant. 'Did you... did you have a drink?'

'No.'

She leaned towards him.

'I only had a small gin with dinner. I'm sorry, I was worried about your mother.'

The smell of alcohol and vomit made her recoil.

'I promise,' he said, 'only one.'

'Are you mad? Where's Varun?' She pushed past him.

'Wait! Wait. Jyoti, wait a minute.' He caught her by the shoulder. 'Listen to me.'

'Let go of me, Praveen.'

'I went to the bathroom five minutes ago. When I came out, the front door was open-'

'What?'

'-and Varun was gone. He's just playing hide-and-seek, that's all. He joked about wanting to play all night.'

'Jo!' Zarina shouted from the car. 'Come help, no? Your mom says she's feeling a little bit dizzy.'

'Give me two minutes,' Praveen said, breathing into her face. 'I'll find him.'

Jyoti clenched her cane. 'You don't know where he is?'

'I'll find him.'

She tried to shake him off but he held on to her.

'Let go of me, Praveen, I won't ask again.'

'I said I'll find him. Why are you acting like this? Just give me two minutes.'

'No.'

'What?'

'I want you to go home. Please.'

'Why? Why would I do that, huh?'

Her shoulder ached where he held her.

'Jyoti, I'm telling you I can help, why aren't you listening to me?'

It didn't make sense. Not once had Varun played a prank on her since they'd brought him to Bangalore. He wouldn't do such a thing. Especially not tonight. Not after seeing his grandmother on the bathroom floor. If anything, he would've stayed up waiting for them to return. Which could only mean Praveen wasn't telling the truth.

'What did you do?' she asked.

'I didn't do anything! I told you, one minute he was in the house, the next the front door was open and he'd bloody run off somewhere.'

'Go home, Praveen.'

'I can help.'

'Okay. Fine. Help me. Do what I'm asking. Go home. Please do that. Let go of me and just go home.' She tried to wriggle out of his grip but he grabbed her swollen wrist. She gasped in pain.

'Why won't you let me help?'

She struggled and he shook her.

'How will you find him without me, huh?'

'Jo!' Zarina shouted from the car. 'What the hell is going on?'

She wrenched herself free but he caught her by the wrist again and her cane fell to the ground as they scuffled with each other. She wanted to slap him across the face, she wanted him gone, out of the way, dead even, anything so that she could hurry inside the house and find Varun. It seemed impossible that this was the same Praveen she'd left behind.

'What will you do without me? How will you look for him when you can't even see? He could be hiding right under your nose and you wouldn't see him. Don't be so stupid. You're blind. You can't do this without me. You need me.'

'Go home,' she said. 'Go home and leave me alone.'

Praveen was breathing heavily. 'I care about you. I'm a good guy. I only want to help. But no, you're like every other woman, so stubborn that you won't accept any help. Fine. It's on your head what happens to the boy now. If he gets run over by a car, it's on your head.'

'Hey!' Zarina shouted. 'I'm at Jyoti's. Can you come over right now? Hurry! There's some guy here who's harassing us and refusing to leave.'

Praveen let go of Jyoti and she rushed inside the house, calling out Varun's name, hoping he hadn't seen anything, and that Praveen had imagined everything in his drunken stupor.

Zarina followed after her. 'Are you okay?' she asked. 'Who was that mental case?'

'Is he gone?'

'Yeah. Not before threatening to break my phone and telling your mom to take care. Can you believe it?'

'Zarina, help me.'

'Will you please tell me what's going on? And your mother is still in the car, by the way.'

'I can't find Varun.'

'What?'

Jyoti barged into the kitchen and out the back door. 'Varun?' she shouted, slipping on the wet grass. It was drizzling. Thunder rumbled overhead. She needed to hurry. Her mind was alight with the sounds and colours of Varun trying to cross the main road.

'Hey! There's a note on your bed,' Zarina shouted.

'Did Varun write it? What does it say? Tell me. Tell me!'

Jyoti had to restrain herself from snatching it out of Zarina's hands. She listened, and as she listened—*Goodbye, Jyoti Aunty*—a fire burned bright in her mind, its flames leaping towards the sky—*I will miss you*—black smoke curling away from the charred chassis of Anu and Alok's wrecked car—*I have gone to be with my parents*—and scattered around the wreckage were shards of glass, reflecting the fire like a thousand glinting eyes.

Zarina was talking about how Varun was such an idiot, what had that fellow done, and asking if they should wait for her husband to help them search, or help her mother first, or maybe call the police.

'Listen to me,' Jyoti said, staring into those thousand glinting eyes and remembering her father lining a boundary wall with cement and the shards of broken bottles, 'I know where he is.'

53

Poppy winced at the hiss and crackle of the tunnel. The opening had widened enough that she could see the ruins of a pavilion on the other side. She was contemplating what to do next when she smelled wisps of smoke and burnt metal, and turned to find the shadow of the man with the plastic bag gliding from tree to tree towards her. She crouched in the long grass and pressed her snout against the earth.

The shadow paused by the entrance to the tunnel. It looked in her direction.

Poppy didn't move. Her body was ready for fight or flight.

Too late, little digger.

It slid through the tunnel, glided across the length of the courtyard, and merged with the shadow of a broken pillar where it seemed to lie in wait.

It was a challenge. Enter at your own peril.

Poppy's heart thudded in her ears. What if the shadow was right and she was too late? What if the tunnel was already feeding on the boy's grief?

Just as she'd guarded the tunnel on this side, now the shadow was guarding the tunnel on the other side. The shadow of the pillar flickered. The same shadow that had crushed her body into the pavement. Overhead, lightning streaked across the sky. Rain started to fall, drops singeing to smoke when they came into contact with the crackling edges of the tunnel.

Poppy scuffed the ground and kept watch, waiting for her chance.

54

Anu watched Alok stack papers on top of the chest of drawers in the hallway. He was trying to tidy the house. From time to time he paused to look at his hands in confusion.

'Will you sit with me?' she asked.

He muttered something to himself but joined her in the living room, still clutching papers, and collapsed into his armchair with his customary groan. It was obvious. Parts of him which she'd forgotten, he'd forgotten, were now returning.

'I want to ask you a question,' she said, 'though it might sound strange.'

'Ask.'

'Do you remember everything?'

His eyes flashed. 'Why?'

She didn't answer.

'At least tell me why.'

'I want to know.'

Silence. She thought about how there existed so many kinds of silence which Jo must've learnt to comprehend. The silence of confusion, anger, tension, guilt, acceptance, calm, restraint, joy. Each with its own distinct texture. She wished she'd spoken with Jo about this.

'Yes,' Alok said at last, 'I remember.'

'Tell me.'

He hunched his shoulders. He crossed his legs and interlinked his fingers. Poor Alok, he was afraid.

'Please tell me,' she asked, gently this time.

'I... why do you want... I mean... okay.' He exhaled. 'I remember the dinner party. And how keen you were to leave as soon as possible. Saying goodbye and getting in the car. Driving back home. The headlights. The headlights and the front of the truck roaring through the windshield.' He covered his eyes with a trembling hand. 'The last sound I heard was you gasping.'

His regret sparked and caught fire. How it blazed through him.

'I'm sorry,' he said.

'It wasn't your fault.'

'So quick. It was so quick. How is it fair? I didn't have a chance. And then... then I was here, in this place, this horrible place, and you were with me.'

It had been the same for her. One moment there'd been glaring lights and a monstrous crunch, and the next moment she was lying on the main road of this place, watching Alok rise and brush grit off his shirt.

'Can I tell you something?' he said. 'I was so relieved to see you then. I was so grateful I could've cried. You were with me. And somehow we were okay. We'd find Varun and everything would be okay.'

The silver in his beard glinted as his face contorted, and she thought about how this place had aged him, thinned his hair, hollowed his cheeks, and yet he was still so handsome.

'Why did you want to know?' he asked.

It was cruel to press him, but she did it anyway. What did cruelty matter to them anymore in this place? 'Do you remember everything from before the accident?'

He frowned. 'Of course, I do.'

'I thought I did too, but I was wrong.'

'I don't understand.'

'I think it started when Varun crossed over from there to here. Couldn't you feel it? We were incomplete, shadows of ourselves. Lost and drifting.'

'Because he wasn't with us.'

'No, that's not it.' She felt like she was inspecting a blown-out circuit, and though she knew what components needed to be taken out and replaced, she had no isopropyl and epoxy for the task at hand. 'When Varun first crossed over, there was only one thought on my mind. To keep him with us.'

'Yes.'

'To be reunited as a family.'

'Exactly.'

'But what if we're wrong?'

'How can we be wrong about that?'

'Alok.'

'No, listen to me, he needs us. He needs *us*. We're his parents. He's our boy.'

'Alok,' she said, giving him a sad smile. 'We're gone.'

For a moment she thought he might explode out of his armchair, but then his body sagged and he looked down at the papers in his hands.

'Have you felt it?' she asked.

'Felt what?'

'A change. Something different.'

He nodded.

'Tell me,' she said.

'What does it matter?'

'Please.'

'What do you want from me, Anu?' he snapped, as he used to snap the countless times when they bickered before.

'Only you, no?' she replied, as she used to reply the countless times she teased him before. It was painful yet thrilling to rediscover their mannerisms.

For a few moments he scrutinized her expression, then he let out a sad little laugh. 'You win.'

'So tell me.'

'So tell you.' He sighed. 'When we first got here, before Varun crossed over, I used to have this dream. I was swimming underwater towards the bottom of a pool where our boy was holding his breath. He was laughing, and bubbles were rising out of his mouth. When I reached out to him, tried to hold him, he swam away from me.'

'And now?'

'And now... Now there's more. It's like I was seeing part of a video. Now I can see him swim between the bodies of other swimmers till someone scoops him up.' He looked at her. 'And it's you. It's you holding him and laughing and threatening to dunk him. Jyoti is splashing about in the shallow end and your mother is sitting in the pavilion, shouting at her to be careful while also giving some poor chap a lecture about how the tea he served was cold.'

Anu smiled. He did too. It was such a beautiful smile, breaking his face open. Tears slid into his beard.

'Summer of last year,' he said in a hoarse whisper. 'When this little house was full to bursting with family.'

Her chest ached at the memory.

'Do you remember how small his hands were? How strong?' he asked. 'I used to sit in this chair and hold him in my arms when he was a baby. It was just me and him. The entire world may have been destroyed, but it didn't matter. He would reach for my face and tug my beard. All I could think of was this is my son. My son. My boy. And I will never let anything bad happen to him.' His face crumpled. 'But something bad did happen, didn't it?'

'Yes.'

He cradled his head in his hands. 'I don't understand. Tell me what's going on. Please, just tell me. What's happening to us?'

'I don't know. I think… I think Varun is filling us with memories, making us whole. We're becoming who we used to be.'

'Who we used to be,' Alok repeated. 'And is that so bad?'

'I don't know. No. I don't think so.'

'We could all be together again. Whole again. We could take care of him.'

'In this place?'

'… Maybe.'

'Would you want that for him?'

'He needs us,' he said, but with little conviction. He looked so lost that she leaned across and slid her hand into his and squeezed. It took him some time to squeeze back, but when he did, it was with both hands curled around hers.

'You were right,' he whispered. 'We should never have gone to that dinner party.'

'Told you. Next time you listen to your wife.'

'She's the boss.'

They sat like that for a long time, holding hands while

Alok wept for all that he'd lost and all that he was regaining. When his tears stopped and his hands no longer painfully clenched her own, he cleared his throat and asked what she'd been waiting for him to ask since she started this conversation: 'What do we do now?'

55

Varun was freezing. Wrapping himself up in his blanket, he climbed out of his cold bed and shuffled down the hallway. Ma and Pa were in the living room, holding hands. His parents had aged. With their stooped shoulders and wispy hair, they looked like a decade had passed through them in a month. When they saw him, Pa shifted in his seat but Ma waved him in and said, 'Come, beta.'

He shuffled into the living room and lay on the carpet.

'You're sweating.' She placed a hand against his neck. 'But you're cold.'

'I'm okay.'

Her face wrinkled with worry and she rubbed his arms.

'I'm sorry, Ma.'

'For what? You haven't done anything wrong.'

'I stopped sitting with you in the park to guess the names of trees.'

'Don't be silly. No need to think about that now.'

'I don't know why I stopped.'

'It's because you're growing up.'

'Remember playing cricket in the park?' Pa said. 'That time when Komal was bowling and the leather ball hit you on the chin? We had to rush to the hospital to get you stitched up! Your mother threatened to beat us black and blue.' He chuckled. 'When we got back home, she said if we ever gave her another scare like that, she'd throw us in the dungeons.'

'The dungeons,' Varun whispered.

'Yes, you both deserved to be locked up,' Ma said.

'But Komal was the one who threw the ball.' He shivered. His body felt heavy and it was a struggle to rearrange his legs. 'Ma, can I have some warm milk?'

Ma and Pa glanced at each other.

'No, I'm so sorry, you can't.'

'Why?'

'You know why, don't you?'

He didn't say anything.

'There's no milk here. No snacks. No food or drink. If you stay here with us–'

'Anu,' Pa warned.

Varun's skin broke into goose pimples. 'You lied to me,' he said.

'No,' Pa said.

'Yes,' Ma said. 'And I'm sorry. We're so sorry.'

'We want what's best for you. You can see that, can't you, beta?' Pa pleaded.

'If I don't eat and drink, then won't I die?'

'Shush!' Pa said. 'Don't say such things.'

'Yes,' Ma said. 'If you don't eat and drink, then you'll die.'

'Like you did.'

Tears spilt from her eyes, down her cheeks, and on to her wrists. He'd made Ma cry. He'd never seen her cry before, and it made him fiercely want to punish her, punish them.

'That uncle said Jyoti Aunty and Grandma don't want me.'

'It sounds like he said some terrible things. But death affects everyone differently. One second you're there, the next you're gone. I told you, sometimes people turn to anger. That doesn't mean you have to forgive him. I won't.'

'Even Pa said Jyoti Aunty would be happier without me.'

Pa fidgeted with the papers on his lap. 'It was wrong of me to have said that. I... I wasn't myself. I'm very sorry.'

'She took care of me.'

'We thought only we could do that.'

'But we know better now,' Ma said.

Varun scratched the bandage on his knee. Its curling edges had browned with dust, but it still held fast to his skin. Jyoti Aunty had promised to return to him. She'd kept him safe in the night, had bought the audiobook so they could listen to the story together.

Ma clapped her hands. 'Come on!' she said, rising. 'Shall I make some tea?'

'Tea?' Pa asked.

'Yes, tea, why are you acting like you've never heard the word before?'

'No, I mean, yes, but...'

'Ma,' Varun whispered, 'you said there was nothing to eat or drink here. Remember?'

'What on earth are you talking about? We just went to the grocery store. We even got some chocolate for you for tonight. Speaking of which, Alok, don't we have to get ready soon? I hope you told them we won't stay for very long.'

'Ma...'

'I know I've already told you this, but just listen once again, okay? I've written our phone numbers on the notepad by the landline. You can call us anytime you want. We'll be back soon anyway, I promise. And don't play with the battery for the gramophone. I'll know if you did!'

'Anu,' Pa said, sheets of paper falling from his lap and scattering across the floor, 'we're gone, remember?'

'What does that mean? And did you put the geyser on? I have to...' she slowed down, 'I have to go... get ready.' Her eyes widened. 'There is no tea, is there?'

'No,' Pa said.

'Because we're gone.'

'I... yes.'

'I forgot. I thought I was... me?'

'What's happening?' Varun asked.

'I don't know,' Pa said. 'I think we're still changing. If you want, we'll become exactly as you remember us.'

'If I want?'

'I need to call Jo,' Ma said, drifting away again. 'I haven't spoken to her all day and she was complaining about Mama driving her nuts. Maybe we should have her stay with us for a while. What do you think?'

Pa looked from Ma to the fallen papers. 'Yes. We're changing. Exactly as you remember us.'

'I don't understand,' Varun said.

'Soon we'll be who we were before we came to this place. We'll have no memory of the accident. And so yes, we'll be exactly as you remember us. We'll be with you, and you'll be with us, together forever.'

Varun pulled the blanket up to his neck. It was hard to understand what Pa was saying, but he could tell there was no joy in Pa's face as he spoke about them being together forever. His eyes were vacant and his voice glum. But why? Why did the idea make him unhappy? They were his parents. Why couldn't they be strong for him?

Ma dropped the telephone and it clattered against the chest of drawers. She ran her hands through her hair, squeezed her head as if it was threatening to burst, then hurried back to the living room and crouched next to Varun. 'Beta, listen to me.'

And suddenly he wanted them to stop.

'I know this is confusing.'

He wanted silence.

'But it's really important you pay attention now.'

His jaw tightened, his chest tightened, and he clenched his fists.

'We're going to help you, okay? But we have to hurry now. You have to listen to me. I know what you're feeling but-'

'NO ONE knows!' he exploded. 'You don't. You DON'T! I'm the one who was left behind, not you!'

'No,' Pa breathed.

'Let him,' Ma said, her face pale and strained.

'You want me to go, but I won't do it. I WON'T! This is my home. Why should I go? Why do you want me to go?'

Pa was shaking his head.

'You do!' Varun choked. 'I know you do! You want me gone.'

Ma waited for him to finish, but Varun could no longer speak and wished they would vanish. Never before had he felt such anger towards them. He remembered sleeping in the dip of their mattress and waiting for them to come back.

'Tell me the truth,' Ma said softly. 'Is this home?'

Varun turned his head away from her.

'I wanted it to be,' she said. 'I wanted everything to go back to the way it was.'

'Same,' Pa said.

'So, you tell us. Is this home? If you think it is, then we'll try, we'll do what you want. This is your decision, not ours.'

Varun struggled to breathe.

'You're right. You were left behind, not us. And we can't know what you've been through. We're sorry. We're so sorry you've had to experience all of this.' Her voice caught. 'I know it sounds impossible right now, but you have to believe me when I say everything will get better. It will. I promise. If you give it a chance. You have to give it a chance, beta. The world exists outside of your grief.'

'How?' Varun asked.

'How what?'

'How can everything get better? You're... you're gone.'

Ma leaned close to him. 'Do you know what your grandma told me and Jo after we lost your grandpa? The people we love are never gone. They stay with us. Here,' she said, touching the side of his head, 'and here,' she said, touching his chest, just above his heart. 'We keep them alive.'

Pa knelt and slipped one hand into Ma's. He reached out for Varun with the other, and Ma did the same. Varun took their hands, larger than his but so familiar, the three of them holding on to each other.

Ma's eyes glimmered. 'Do you understand, beta? Letting go is not the end.'

And Varun felt something vast and enormous crumble within him as he whispered, 'Okay.'

The lightbulb in the lamp flickered and then popped. As did the lights in the house.

'Time to leave,' said Pa.

'Are you ready?' Ma asked. In the darkness, the question

transported Varun back to wintry school mornings, the house filled with the deep blues of dawn, scrambling to get ready before the first rays of the sun. He would take a scalding hot bucket bath while Ma packed lunch. They would walk out of the colony together, their every exhalation a plume of white.

'It's so dark,' Pa said.

Varun remembered what Jyoti Aunty had given him. He climbed out of the blanket and, ignoring the aching cold, turned the torch on. The beam of light cut bright against the darkness.

'We're with you,' Ma said. 'Show us the way.'

Pa opened the door. The streets were empty, the buildings crowded close, and electrical cables criss-crossed the sky, dangling from telephone posts in coiled loops. All was silent save for the pitter-patter of rain. They bumped into one another as they moved through the colony and climbed over the rubble. Ma and Pa kept glancing at each other and behind them, as though expecting something to leap out of the shadows. Varun waved the torch ahead of him, guiding the narrow beam of light up the side of a building.

'Keep the light on the path, beta,' Pa said. 'This place is such a mess. The last thing we need right now is to trip over some collapsed house.'

'Careful,' Ma said, 'if we come across any ruins then your Pa will want to stop and inspect them.'

Varun chuckled. 'He'll give us a lecture.'

'Lodi-era monuments and the threat of unchecked urban development.'

'Hey, that's a very real concern!' Pa protested.

'Our forgotten buildings. They carry important historical information on the last dynasty of the Delhi Sultanate.'

'A snapshot,' Varun said, stamping his feet with delight.

'Oh yes, they're a snapshot of history that we must strive to preserve. Remember, Munirka was one of the first villages to be urbanized in the fifties. And see what it looks like now!'

The three of them laughed. Because it was true, that's exactly what Pa used to say. How easy it would be to stay here, actually, Varun thought. What did darkness and shadows matter when his parents were, by his side, laughing and holding hands? And it was then, when they'd reached the gate of the colony and the main road was in sight, that Ma's grip lightened.

'It's okay, isn't it?' Pa asked Ma.

'Yes,' she said. 'It's okay, he'll be okay.'

They kissed, their smiles tinged with sadness.

'What are you doing?' Varun asked.

'Sorry, beta,' Pa said.

His parents were fading.

'Wait. What are you doing?'

'I'm so sorry.'

'Wait, wait. No, please wait! Ma! Stop!' He tried to grab at her sleeves but his hands went through her. 'Don't go. Please don't go. I don't want you to go. I don't. I don't.'

'We know,' Ma said. 'We don't want to go either. We never did. All we wanted was to grow old with you, watch you live your life.' The outlines of her hands cupped his face. 'Remember, letting go is not the end.'

Pa was first. He thumped his chest and said, 'My boy.'

Ma was next. Her final words were soft, in snatches, like fog lifting between the branches of trees:

                Your
       fathe
                              nd
                 I
                       ve
you
              lways
                          We
                               love
                     you
            beta

They were gone. The street was empty. 'Ma?' Varun shouted, his voice shrill. 'Pa?' He wiped his cheeks. Why did they go? They could've stayed here. Even as he thought that he had a vision of the bungalow in Bangalore with its windows glowing a warm yellow in the night. Would he have wanted Ma and Pa to stay in this place of shadows?

His legs ached, as though he'd been running for hours. He looked back a last time, then crossed the street, and entered the courtyard. The beam of his torch led the way as he hurried to the wall. There was nothing for him here now.

The air behind him hissed and crackled.

He turned, holding the torch in front of him like a sword. Within the shadows of the pavilion stood the silhouette of a boy, the same boy who'd stood in the corner of his room. The next instant it was a woman, then a man, then it vanished, and the shadow of the pillar lengthened. It glided across the broken tiles of the pool, moving towards him with a swiftness that was otherworldly.

Varun ran.

>What did you do?

He gasped and stumbled.

>What did you DO?

If he could reach the wall, he'd have a chance, he could escape. The hole was only a few feet away. There was the grove, the bougainvillea. He was so close!

>Watch, little digger.

Something grabbed at his ankle.

'No!' he screamed.

>Watch me take him from you.

Something grabbed at his collar.

>Watch me take the light in his eyes.

The whole world tilted.

>Save him if you can.

Lightning streaked across the sky, there was the boom of thunder, and Varun heard deep echoing rumbles of laughter as something wrapped its hands around his neck and brought him crashing headfirst to the floor.

56

Poppy was afraid to move. The smell of orange bitterness was sharp in her snout, and above her the vertical seam of the tunnel was no longer crackling and hissing but spitting in anger, its edges ablaze in the rain as it seemed to contract. There were sounds coming from behind her as well, but before she could do anything bright sparks flashed away from the tunnel to scorch nearby trees. Smoke rose from the branches.

She was out of time. The boy had taken the bait and the tunnel was closing.

But then she saw him. He was hurrying towards the hole, waving a beam of light in front of him. He was unharmed and coming back! And right when she allowed herself to believe everything would be okay, the shadow of the pillar moved.

Poppy howled.

She leapt out of the grass and charged at the tunnel, but flames billowed from its edges and singed her fur.

Watch, little digger.

She snarled, unable to do anything as the boy ran towards her and the tunnel narrowed and the shadow descended upon him.

Watch me take him

No.

Watch me take the light in his eyes.
He wasn't going to make it.
Save him if you can.

The shadow struck the boy. He fell, landing with a muffled thump by the wall. The shadow laughed, rumbling like stones scraping against each other. The tunnel sputtered, twisting and lashing against itself. Poppy bared her teeth and prepared to leap across and die defending the lives of her family.

Her nose twitched. Her ears pricked. What was that? She could hear others in the grove, thrashing through the undergrowth, calling to each other, calling for the boy. But they were moving in the wrong direction.

She barked.

Maybe there was time.

As loudly as she could, as though her life depended on it, Poppy barked.

Help!

Help!

Help!

He's here!

Look. This is the swimming pool where you learnt to swim. The air smells of chlorine and the water is cool and clear. The concrete of the diving board is warm against the soles of your bare feet. In the deep end is a 50 paisa waiting to be found.

Look. This is the park where you and Ma guessed the names of trees. Drifting across the sky are diamond kites tugging at their lines. In time, nasturtiums will gather and bloom around the stone benches. Stray dogs will nose your palms for treats.

Look. This is Munirka. This is the rooftop where you and Komal shared snacks and pretended to be watchful spies. Down the alley is the parking lot where you played seven stones and Pa taught you how to roller-skate, tying your laces for you, and picking you up every time you fell.

Look. This is your home. Your silver-star painting of a lizard hangs above your bed, and the gramophone you and Ma made is in the living room. Sitting on a bookshelf is Pa's coin album. The television plays cartoons and the portable heater turns on with a click.

Everything is as you remember it. Everything. You will-

'No.'

You will stay here and grow old with-

'Don't! They're gone.'

But this is what you have wanted. Ever since that night

==when you lay in their bed, hiding under their blanket, waiting for the door to unlock. And you can have it all.==

'I need to go back.'

He could feel the stone tiles pressing against his face. His arms were painfully heavy. He couldn't lift them, couldn't move, when that was what he wanted most. To stand up. To go back.

==There is no one waiting for you on the other side, remember?==

'Stop.'

==You made their lives miserable. They don't want you.==

'That's not true.'

==They hate you.==

'Please.'

==She wishes you were dead!==

'Please!' Varun screamed. 'Just let me go. Please.' He could hear barking in the distance, voices calling out his name.

==Stay here. You'll have everything you want here.==

He could feel the rough metal ridges of the torch in his hand. It was a gift from Jyoti Aunty. He remembered her striking a match and showing him how to light a candle to keep the darkness at bay.

==Stay. Don't leave.==

Rain was pouring down. Poppy was nearby, barking. There was a flash of lightning, an explosion of thunder, followed by a great crack and splintering of wood. It was like the world was ending. He concentrated as hard as he could.

==Don't.==

He gritted his teeth and twisted, kicked, and slowly, as though wrestling an impossible force, he rose to his feet. His eyes flicked open. The torch's narrow beam of light illuminated the hole in the wall. 'I'm sorry,' he said, his voice trembling, 'I need to go home.'

This is home.

Varun couldn't say the words. He only shook his head.

A great weight lifted from his shoulders. He scrambled to the hole in the wall and was halfway through, one foot planted on the damp earth of the other side, when the hair on his neck stood on end. There was a pull. The air sizzled. He turned. The shadow was once again a boy. A boy that looked just like him. And then, in the blink of an eye, the shadow knifed across the courtyard to pierce him clean in the chest, just above the heart.

Varun fell.

58

Despite the splitting pain in her head, Usha checked and rechecked all of the rooms in the house. Even her bathroom. She looked under the beds and she swung open cupboards and trunks. But Varun wasn't there. Where could he have gone? She remembered a night from decades ago when Anu had snuck out and returned home at some unearthly hour stinking of cigarettes and booze.

There was an empty glass lying on the carpet. Praveen had stumbled down the driveway, muttering curses at them. A drunk bully, a small man, just like his father. Skin prickling with anger, she picked up the glass, rinsed it, and left it to dry on the counter.

She peered out the screen door at the back garden. Jyoti had insisted she stay behind because someone needed to be at home. Zarina had insisted she stay behind because she needed to rest. She scratched her scalp, tempted to remove the bandage and explore the newly formed ridges of her stitched skin. The truth was that she did need to be careful. It would've been foolish to run around in the rain right now. What if her stitches tore open? When she woke up in the hospital emergency room, her first thoughts had streaked towards Jyoti and Varun, Anu and Alok, Poppy, and this house she'd lived in for more than thirty years of her life. Jyoti's hands had grasped at her own, and she'd felt their strength. Strength despite everything that had happened.

Trees swayed with the wind, their leaves glittering silver and white. Rain was falling steadily now. The sky occasionally lit up with lightning. Hurry, she thought as she watched the grove, waiting for the shadows to part, and for Jyoti and Varun to return to her. Hurry.

59

Jyoti slipped. The ground was slushy and her cane kept knocking against tree trunks or hard knotted roots. There was no time to waste, but the deeper she went inside the grove, the more obstacles she encountered. Trailing branches raked her hair. Thorns pricked her ankles. She slipped again and cursed the grove. It had gone from a place of adventure with Anu to an ominous forbidden territory, before taking root in golden-lit nostalgia. But this was an altogether different reality.

'Varun?' she called out.

She was drenched. What about Varun? Was he huddled under some tree, catching his death from the cold, or had he already climbed the boundary wall and was now halfway across the city? She was so stupid to have left him behind. What if Praveen was right? Here she was, scrambling through the grove like a lunatic, and if she couldn't find Varun then it truly would be on her head.

'Jo!' Zarina shouted some fifteen feet to her right.

'Did you find him? Is he okay?'

'No. No sign of him.'

'Keep searching.'

'Are you sure?'

She heard the doubt in Zarina's voice and pushed forward.

Her cane struck something, but in her rush she ran right into the boundary wall. Clutching her shoulder, she tried hard not to make a sound.

'Hey! What was that? Did you fall?'

'I'm fine, I'm fine.'

'Are you okay?'

She squeezed her cane so tight in her fists that it hurt. 'Varun?' she bellowed. 'Can you hear me? Answer me!' She was repeating words Mama had used countless times before when looking for her and Anu. 'Answer me right now or you'll be in deep trouble. I'm not fooling around. It's time to go home.'

'Jo!' Zarina shouted, heading in her direction.

She slid her hand along the surface of the boundary wall and followed it away from her friend. If need be, she would follow the damned thing across the entire property till she found Varun and gave him a good beating for making her worry so much.

'Jo! Wait!'

But she couldn't wait, she couldn't stop.

'We need to go back! He's not out here.'

She half-jogged, half-ran, tripping over roots but somehow keeping her balance. Zarina caught up with her. She didn't grab her by the wrist like Praveen had, nor did she clutch her shoulder or wrestle with her.

'Jo, I'm sorry, I don't think he's out here.'

Jyoti slowed her pace but continued to stagger forward. All the energy in her legs was leaking away. Zarina walked beside her till she finally stopped.

'Let's go back,' Zarina said. 'We'll regroup.'

How could she return without Varun?

'We'll find him, I'm telling you.'

She'd promised to be back soon. He'd made her promise.

'That's it. There you go.' Zarina pulled her into a gentle hug and she clutched her friend who was bony yet strong. When Zarina spoke, her words hummed in both of their ribcages. 'We'll find him, okay? We'll find him.'

Jyoti's knees trembled. She was about to ask how, she was about to give up when she heard a dog bark.

'You ready?' Zarina asked.

'Shush!'

'What?'

'Shush! Wait a second.'

She stood still, concentrating on the sounds in the grove. There! There it was again! Poppy was barking like she was possessed, like she was howling for the dead, and Jyoti took off in her direction.

'Jo!' Zarina shouted.

Jyoti ran, the fastest she'd ever run since losing her eyesight. She tripped over a tree root and fell, and even though the breath was knocked out of her and pain flared in her jaw and left leg, she got up and limped forward. She rammed her shoulder against a tree trunk but kept going. Her cane fell but it no longer mattered.

'Poppy?' she called out. There was a strong smell of burnt wood in the air. 'Poppy? Oh, Poppy, I'm here. Shush.' She knelt by the side of the dog, who was whining and yelping and running in circles around her, and she patted the ground frantically till at last her hand grasped a small shoe, a leg, a body, and the face of her boy. The world contracted. Her sense of hearing diminished. There was darkness, silence, and the cold curve of Varun's jaw. She struggled to sit him upright and cradle him against her chest. She rubbed his arms. She knew she was speaking his name, but she couldn't hear her words. In this vacuum, she was waiting.

He groaned.

The world cracked and sounds bled in.

He groaned again. 'I'm sorry, Jyoti Aunty,' he whispered.

The world came rushing back in. The rain, the wind in the leaves, Poppy howling and Zarina moving around her, asking if he was alright and exclaiming nonstop that she couldn't believe it and how dumb was this boy and what was he even doing here in the middle of nowhere. Jyoti draped his arms around her neck. They were deathly cold. But they moved, they wrapped around her neck and held on to her. It was all she needed. She took a breath and stood up with Varun in her arms.

'Zarina, let's go home.'

'Can you manage?'

'I can manage.'

Her friend placed a hand on her shoulder. Together they walked through the grove, Jyoti carrying Varun in her arms. No matter what, she wouldn't let him fall.

60

The house was still. There was the steady drone of the fridge, the occasional snore from Grandma's bedroom. It was early morning and Varun rustled under the blanket. He didn't want to wake Jyoti Aunty, who'd unrolled a thin mattress over the carpet by his bed and stayed with him throughout the night. But when he checked on her, he found her eyes were open, her head tilted towards him.

'You okay?' she asked.

'Yeah.'

'Liar. Do you need anything?'

'Water?'

She rose, wrapped herself in sheets, and poured him a glass of water. He drank it in one swallow and collapsed back into his pillows. His chest was aching from where the shadow had struck him. Jyoti Aunty sat on the side of the bed. The mattress dipped slightly from her weight, pulling him close to her.

'How do you feel?'

'Tired.'

'Feverish?'

'No.'

'Well, touch wood you haven't caught anything.'

He knocked on the frame of the bed with his knuckles. She didn't smile. She asked him the question he'd been dreading since returning to the bungalow.

'Varun, what happened?'

He turned on his side.

'I know you're tired. I won't push you. But at least tell me, that man who was here, did he say anything to you? Did he hurt you or... do anything to you?'

'No.'

'Are you sure? You won't be in trouble.'

'Yes.'

'You promise?'

Varun thought of Uncle Praveen slumped in the living room chair, the empty glass slipping from his hand. 'He sounded sad. That's all. I don't remember everything he said. But he sounded sad. He kept asking me, wouldn't it be nice if we could have our lives back?'

'He didn't shout at you?'

'No.'

'Is that why you left? And why you wrote that note? Because of what he said?'

'I don't know.'

'That note. What did you mean by it?'

'I don't know, Jyoti Aunty. I'm sorry.'

'I was so worried.'

She took his hand. She traced his fingertips with her thumb, pushed her thumb down against the flat of his fingernails, and he knew this was a gesture of hers that was as natural as kissing him on the cheek.

'Whenever your mother and I were late coming home from school,' Jyoti Aunty said, 'your grandmother would give us a good shouting. *Who told you to come back so late, huh? Look at the time! You horrible children, giving me a heart attack!*' She gave a sad little laugh. 'Your mother and I loved giving her tension.

Terrible, no? But we found it funny. Plus, we knew she was just playing with us. If she was actually angry, then we'd run for our lives. Your grandfather included.'

Varun chuckled.

She patted his hand. 'Any time you want to talk to me, beta, about anything, you can. You can tell me anything. I promise. I god promise, okay? You don't have to be afraid.'

'Okay.'

'Good.'

He wasn't sure what to say, so he said the truth. 'I wanted to see Ma and Pa.'

'Oh.'

'I know I shouldn't have gone so late in the night, but that's why I went.'

'You went looking for them in the grove?'

He shook his head. 'Through the wall.'

'You climbed over the wall?'

'No. I went through it. And on the other side was Delhi. And Munirka.'

'But you didn't climb over the wall, right? You didn't cut yourself on the glass?'

'No, Jyoti Aunty.'

'Okay, sorry, just checking. So, you went to Munirka?'

'Never mind.'

'No, tell me. Please. I'm sorry.'

'It's okay.'

'I'm listening. I promise. You went to Munirka, and then what happened?'

'It was Munirka, but it also wasn't. I went back home and saw Ma and Pa. I thought they'd be happy to see me and I could stay with them in the old house.' He remembered the outlines of Ma's fingers cupping his face, her words fading into thin air. 'But I can't. Everything's changed, and they're gone now.'

His throat tightened. It was difficult to speak, to breathe.

Jyoti Aunty shifted closer to him. For an instant he wanted to run away again, or for her to leave. But then she took his arm, lifted him up, and pulled him into a hug. She rocked him like he was a baby and hummed a soft tune in his ear, similar to the one that Grandma and Ma used to hum when he was smaller, and limb by limb, bone by bone, Varun let go. New aches announced themselves, but his body finally relaxed. He rested his head on her shoulder and breathed.

'Together,' Jyoti Aunty murmured. 'It'll take time, but we'll get through it together. Promise.'

He wasn't sure what she meant by that but he didn't worry. He let her ease him back into the pillows and tuck him under the blanket. She gently combed his hair with her fingertips, like Ma did, and his scalp tingled, as though the blood in his body recognized blood of its own, and rushed to meet at the point of contact.

Varun slipped into a sleep that was free of dreams.

EPILOGUE

Jyoti listened to the traffic. She stood up when a bus screeched to a halt by the side of the road, and moved forward when she heard children clamber down its stairs and shout cries of farewell to their friends.

'Hi, Jyoti Aunty,' Varun said, taking her hand.

'How was it, all okay?'

'Yeah.'

'No problems?'

'Nope.'

'Good. Did you make any new friends?'

'Oh, come on,' he said, dragging the syllable of the last word. She let him lead, heeding his warnings whenever there was an obstacle. She would've preferred to use her cane, especially since the municipal corporation was at last digging up the road to install new pipes and repair old connections, but this was a learning process for both of them. Patience was required. Hopefully, pain wouldn't be involved. When the bus rumbled past and they were out of earshot of the other school children, he said, 'We didn't really have any classes today. There was an orientation assembly, and then we met the teachers and collected our textbooks. We also had to go over the timetable.'

'Still sounds like a busy day.'

'Our science teacher talked a little bit about the syllabus. We're going to be learning about refraction and reflection later in the year. She said it was related to eyesight.'

'Very interesting. And your classmates? What are they like?'

'They're okay, I guess.'

'No bullies, no?'

'I don't think so.'

'Anyone you like?'

He was silent. His shoes scraped the pavement. She worried she might've crossed a line asking the same question in different ways, but then his little hand gripped hers tighter. 'They all know each other already. I'm the only new student in my class.'

'Oh,' she said, squeezing back with a mingling sense of relief and worry. 'That's okay. It's your first day. Give it some time and you'll get to know them and they'll get to know you.'

He didn't say anything.

'Listen,' she said, 'Rukmini went through the same thing when she first started attending classes at the AFB.'

'Really?'

'Yes, and now I can barely get her and her friends to shut up in class.'

'She told me she liked your class most.'

'Sweet girl, but she's one hundred percent lying. She loves PE.'

'Can she come over today?'

'I think it's too late to ask her, but maybe we could invite her over the weekend? What do you think? After your swimming lessons?'

'Cool.'

'Yes, cool. Very cool.' She wondered what new slang she'd

eventually have to learn to keep up with him. 'Did you finish your lunch?'

'Yeah...'

She caught the hesitation in his voice. 'But?'

'Nothing.'

'What happened?'

'I hurt myself.'

'Already?'

'I didn't mean to.'

'While eating lunch?'

'No, during lunch break.'

'What happened?'

'Some of the seniors were playing cricket and they asked me if I wanted to join them. I fell on my chin diving to catch the ball. But it was an accident.'

'An accident! How on earth is it an accident if you're deliberately diving face-first into the ground to catch a ball?'

'I had to, Jyoti Aunty! It was such a good catch.'

'I should give you a whack.' She stopped and reached for his chin.

'I'm fine.' He tried to squirm away.

She expected to find a pulpy wad of tissues soggy with blood, but there was just a bandage and nothing else. The school nurse had done a neat job. 'Did the chin split? Is there a cut or a scrape?'

'Scrape.'

'You should be more careful.'

'But you didn't even listen to me! It was such a good catch-'

She exhaled in mock exasperation.

'-that one of the seniors told me to sign up for the school team's trials.'

'Great. More horrors to look forward to.'

Varun ignored her and continued to chatter away about the game and how close it was and how one senior cheated and the others belted him. Jyoti smiled to herself. A month had passed since Mama's accident and she'd come home to find Varun missing. She wasn't expecting miracles, but it was a relief that at least on his first day of school there was a sense of loss replaced by gain.

As they headed down the road leading home, her field of hearing expanded.

'Ow! Jyoti Aunty, you're squeezing too tight.'

'Sorry, sorry.'

She pretended everything was fine but tripped twice. Her heart hammered in her throat and she struggled to make sense of sounds when Varun opened the gate.

'Are you okay?' he asked.

'I'm fine.' She pinched his ear. Mama kept harping on about how Varun resembled Alok, but Jyoti was convinced he'd inherited Anu's features. It was always a pleasant surprise to find Anu in the curl of his ear or the bridge of his nose. 'Why don't you go on? Your grandmother cut some fruit for you.'

'Okay, bye!'

He ran down the driveway, his backpack slinging back and forth across his shoulders, and the spoon in his empty lunch box rattling with his every step. It was a good sound, like a bell ringing at the end of a long school day.

She latched the gate and then locked it with a heavy padlock. This was a recent precaution, one she'd insisted on taking after someone had bumped into her on the road and grabbed her by the wrist to say, 'Sorry, Jyoti.' He hadn't responded when she called his name, but when she called his number, his phone had rung some ten feet behind her. Rumour had it he was engaged. If that was true, it hadn't stopped Praveen from haunting her footsteps this past month. His parents were no longer in touch with Mama, though his father had sent a message asking her not to spread malicious lies about his son if she knew what was good for her.

There were moments, like now, when she went over their conversations and wondered if she'd suspected anything. Unlikely, because she'd trusted him to watch Varun. Yet hadn't she tried to get Mrs Naronha and Zarina to cover for her as well?

Jyoti rattled the gate. It held firm.

The last thing she wanted was any trouble. Of course, that was unlikely considering Varun was hell-bent on throwing himself head first into the ground every opportunity he got. Not one day at school and he'd already had his chin patched up. He probably knew the school nurse by name. They'd be best friends, for sure. At least there were no more incidents in the grove now. For a while, she and Zarina had extended their evening walks to the boundary wall, which they'd inspected for signs of damage, cracks, or holes through which Varun might climb through to the other side. But there was nothing. The wall was intact. The only sign of damage was to a tree that had been struck by lightning, its trunk split in two.

Her phone pinged. She listened to a voice message from Zarina.

Good luck with your boring class! Why don't you and the family come over for dinner Wednesday night? I'm going to make some dhansak. Let me know. And has mister brat started reading the book I gave him or not yet?

Before she could reply, her phone pinged again.

Tara wants to know what time you and mister brat are going over to the art studio.

Before she could reply, there was yet another ping. No message, just the sound of a kiss.

Jyoti walked back home, smiling, thinking to herself that despite all its difficulties, there was still plenty of joy in this life.

'Here,' Usha said as Jyoti stepped inside. She took the cane from Jyoti's hand, and handed her a cup of tea and a bowl of fruit. 'Now, I know your very important class for your very important course is about to begin, but just give me one second. Seema cooked brinjal for tonight. She left early to attend an appointment with her husband. Rakesh is fine, don't worry, it was just a follow-up. But because she left early, Seema didn't clean your room.'

'Mama, that's fine.'

'I'm just telling you, that's all.'

'Okay.'

'Varun is talking to that friend of his from Delhi, that Komal girl. Who, by the way, might be visiting Bangalore over summer break. That'll be nice for him. Anyway, he's asked if he can play outside for an hour because there's no homework today, which is perfect. That'll give you some peace and quiet. Esther is coming over, but we'll have our tea outside. And that fool of a lawyer called. He wants us to meet him Saturday morning at ten.'

'At ten?'

'Yes. What's the problem?'

'How are we going to do that?'

'Why?'

'Varun and I signed up for swimming lessons, remember?'
'You never told me.'
'It's on the list!'
'What nonsense.'
'Did you check the list on your phone?'
'You never told me about it.'
'Mama, I shared it with you. I said-'
'Fine, fine, fine. I'll call the swim coach and try to reschedule. God only knows if that's possible.'
'Next time, check the list first.'
Usha clicked her tongue.
'Thanks, Mama.'
'Go. Your class will be starting soon.'
'I'm not some child, you know.' Jyoti balanced the bowl on top of her cup and slid her free hand along the wall down the hall to her bedroom.

The next time, Usha thought, she would leave the tea and fruit on her table.

'Here!' she shouted, clapping her hands at Poppy. 'Enough barking. Go on, get out!' She opened the kitchen screen door and watched Varun and Poppy race into the back garden. She glanced at the clock. It was nearly five. Esther would be here any moment with more fascinating news about her phone connection and how the municipal corporation fellows had damaged the pavement and lopped off the branches of her tree. The last point did rankle. Maybe it was time for her to rejoin the residents' association, get them to do something useful for once.

She could hear Jyoti speaking with her teacher. Jyoti had of course been unable to attend the course in Thiruvananthapuram, but when she resumed work at the

AFB, that Hema woman had enrolled her in a long-distance learning module on empowering the blind. It ate into Jyoti's time, but she didn't complain. The opposite in fact. She spoke for hours on end with Zarina about pursuing new policies to campaign for in the coming year.

Like Anu, Jyoti persevered. Her daughters were strong. It was a good truth.

Usha went to her bathroom, which the plumber had recently repaired for an outrageous fee. The generator too had been replaced. Their savings had taken quite a beating, but it was worth it. Now they needed to paint the walls and chase away all the spiders and silverfish. There was still plenty to do.

As Usha changed into something decent for company, and Jyoti listened to the electronically warped voice of her teacher on her laptop, Varun and Poppy walked through the grove.

Poppy knew where they were going but she allowed him this final journey. There lingered in the boy's wake faint traces of bitter orange rinds, joined now by other new smells, like that of the calcium tablets her ma took, of tender green shoots gently parting soil. Blinking in the day's last rays of sunlight, she listened to the hum of insects in her territory and was content.

Varun clenched his toes in his shoes when he spotted the bougainvillea. He plucked three bracts for the jug in the living room. The wall hadn't changed. Lizards skittered across its cracked surface, little ghosts watchful for signs of danger. And there was the hole. He knelt to look across, not knowing what to expect.

The courtyard was there, covered in a fine layer of dust. Beyond lay the empty pool and the pavilion with its broken pillar. He shuddered at the memory of the shadow. How it had looked like him, scared and alone, before slicing through him. If he crossed over, he knew he would be enveloped by that silence once more. Everything still lay in ruins.

Houses change after people die.

Maybe it was true for places as well. If he flew to Delhi and visited Munirka, the actual Munirka, he knew the pool, the park, the colony, and his home would no longer be the same for him. There would be an emptiness, a fragility. No matter how hard he wished for it to be the same, that old connection was broken.

There was an ache in his chest, which made him wince. He unbuttoned his shirt and inspected the two bruises just above his heart where the shadow had struck him. But they weren't bruises. He'd thought they were, but they weren't sensitive to touch. They neither hurt nor faded away with time. When he'd shown them to Grandma, she'd said they were birthmarks. Jyoti Aunty had mistaken his silence for sadness and consoled him, telling him they were not uncommon. But he'd been thinking of Pa, his forearm and the ink blot.

Poppy sniffed the roots of a tree nearby.

It was a surprise. He'd expected the place to not be here anymore. Maybe, like Ma had said, it was up to him.

If he wanted, he could go across and explore for five minutes, maybe even ten. But he thought instead about Jyoti Aunty and Grandma and the feeling he got when he returned from school and caught sight of the driveway. Slowly, piece by piece, bricks remade themselves till the hole was smoothed from existence and all that was left was the wall, sagging and chipped. He took the coin from his pocket and used it to mark three lines. Two were parallel with each other, while the third connected them. No matter how temporary they were, it felt good to hold on to this idea of a doorway back to Munirka.

He left the coin by the base of the doorway.

We'll get through it together. Promise.

He was beginning to understand what Jyoti Aunty had meant. On Saturday she was taking him swimming. Hopefully, Rukmini could join them after. On Wednesday they'd be going to the arts studio. Jyoti Aunty had been teaching him how to use the pottery wheel and though he still made a mess, he could see now what she meant when she said it was a kind of magic, using your imagination to create something out of nothing. And tonight, he, Grandma, and Jyoti Aunty were going to listen to the audiobook of a story that used to be a favourite of Ma's.

He couldn't wait.

It was time to go home, but before he left, he placed his hand on the doorway and whispered to the cracked surface, to the place beyond the wall, to Ma and Pa, 'Goodbye.'

ACKNOWLEDGEMENTS

It took me three years to write this odd little book. During this period many people set aside time to read drafts, share feedback, double-check facts, or simply listen to me as I went on and on like a lunatic about abandoned plotlines and characters. This book wouldn't be what it is without them.

Thank you to Aathira Menon, Aldeena Raju, Molly Majumder, Molly Morris, Rowan Whiteside, and everyone else who read early drafts and nudged me in the right direction.

Special thanks to four of my closest friends – Amulya Shruthi, Hiteshi Mehta, James Kanjamala, and Mahreen Sohail. Amulya is hilariously honest with me and belts me whenever I write something terrible. James is an editor extraordinaire who does everything he can to help a book succeed. Hiteshi drilled it into me that stories need masala. And Mahreen, one of the finest writers I know, has helped me navigate many identity and writing crises.

My Uncle Jogi, who started to lose his vision in his forties, played a big role in shaping this book. He took me to the National Association for the Blind in Delhi and introduced me to Mr Mukesh Sharma, the director at the time. Mr Mukesh Sharma and the staff gave me a tour of their facilities, allowed me to sit in on one of their classes, and candidly answered my many questions. I'll always be grateful to them.

I also owe much to Dr M. Leona Godin and her column, A Blind Writer's Notebook, published by *Catapult*.

I have quoted the epigraphs to Chapters 1 and 31 of *Watership Down* by Richard Adams. My parents used to read the book to me when I was a child, and in many ways it's what led to me falling in love with both reading and writing.

Thank you to Hemali Sodhi and Ambar Sahil Chatterjee at A Suitable Agency for championing my book and finding it a great home. Poor Ambar! I must've asked him a thousand questions, but he answered all of them and was always patient, kind, and supportive.

Thank you to Hachette, especially Poulomi Chatterjee and Swarnima Narayan who worked on my book.

And to the person who has been there with me from the start, who encouraged me to have fun and write without care in notebooks, who listened to me express my doubts and fears and frustrations over the years, and still, for some bizarre reason, agreed to marry me – thank you, Dani. Home is where you are. *Meju*.

Lastly, dear reader, thank you for reading my book.